STUFFED

STUFFED

LIZ BRASWELL

DI**SN**E**P** • HYPERION

Los Angeles   New York

This book is for
Alex and Ivy
and Dylan and Max and Maddy and Ness and Xavier
and everyone who still sleeps with a Stuffy
because of the Monsters

First Hardcover Edition, November 2019
First Paperback Edition, April 2021
10 9 8 7 6 5 4 3 2 1
FAC-025438-21050
Printed in the United States of America

This book is set in Jensen Recut/Fontspring; Cooper, Scratch,
Neutraface Txt, Helvetica LT Pro/Monotype
Designed by David Hastings and Tyler Nevins

Library of Congress Control Number for Hardcover: 2018043395
ISBN 978-1-368-04535-3
Visit www.DisneyBooks.com

SUSTAINABLE
FORESTRY
INITIATIVE
Certified Chain of Custody
Promoting Sustainable Forestry
www.sfiprogram.org
SFI-01054
The SFI label applies to the text stock

From the very first day the sun rose over the world there have been shadows;

For where there is Light, there is always Dark.

Humans and their friends play in the Light of the sun

But there are Monsters who lurk in the Darkness, waiting to grab them.

What follows is one tale in the eternal war against the Dark.

It is the story of a small boy, and his even smaller guardian.

So, by the Grace of the Velveteen, our story begins.

A Package Arrives

"Bob? Booooobb! There's a package for you!"

The doorbell hadn't been rung, and the quick footsteps of the postwoman couldn't be heard as she trotted away from the house and back to the safety of her truck. If Mrs. Smith hadn't been opening the door to check on the whimsical spring weather, the brown cardboard box might have sat there all day.

"I think it's from your parents!"

She pulled the box inside and the whole Smith family gathered around it: Mrs. and Mr. and their children, Clark and Anna. The handwriting on the package was deliberate and neat, the return stamp from California. Unmistakably Grandma and Grandpa Smith. Sometimes they sent postcards from the beach or oranges from their backyard tree. There was something decidedly *not* fresh and beachy about this strange box, however.

Mr. Smith frowned and then went to work ripping off the

old-fashioned paper tape. When he finally managed to open the flaps, a musty, mildewed puff of air exploded out of it.

"Whoa," Anna said, leaning over to look.

Inside were bits and pieces of Mr. Smith's childhood, dun-colored and worn. There was a paperweight, a plastic spaceship, some books without covers, a few weird little figurines.

Mrs. Smith reached in and deftly took out a letter, the only recent object in the pile.

"*Going through some old stuff—thought you'd like to have them.* Oh. That's . . . nice." Mrs. Smith was a very neat person and liked things that smelled of lemons, not mildew.

"Oh cool! Can I look at them?" Clark asked, reaching in to grab the figurines.

But Mr. Smith was regarding the items with a look less like *delight* and more like *dawning horror.* His eyes were very far away.

"Let's leave your dad alone for a few minutes to go through this stuff by himself," Mrs. Smith suggested gently. "He'll call you when he's ready to share."

Disappointed but unprotesting, Clark and Anna followed her glumly out of the room, leaving their father with the box.

He didn't move for a long time.

Finally he reached in with reluctant hands and picked up a single object—the paperweight.

The thing that was under it rose up like a coil of smoke.

Less surprised than resigned, Mr. Smith didn't even cry out when it descended on him.

ONE

Night

Tomorrow, summer began.

Tomorrow, summer stretched three green months into the future, wide and open like a storybook landscape.

Or like a Monopoly board with the months in one pleasant block, waiting for hotels.

Fourth grade ended tomorrow. A nearly infinite sunny time approached for Clark, full of:

Reading as many books as he wanted.

Playing in the backyard until he was called in.

Afternoons at the pool and, if he was lucky, sometimes the lake.

Time would be marked by meals, not bells. And meals would sometimes be picnics or surprise outings to the Tastee-Freez.

Most importantly, summer meant the longest days and the *shortest nights.*

But all that began tomorrow.

Right now it was still tonight.

And night was creeping in.

Mrs. Smith speared a ravioli on her fork, a bright grin on her face. "*SO!* Tomorrow. Last day of school. What next, team? What are your big plans for June, July, and August?"

Clark's sister, Anna, rolled her heavily made-up eyes and nudged him in the stomach with her elbow. She was sixteen but mostly treated him like an equal. Clark rolled his eyes back at her. It was a nice distraction from watching the light fade beyond the windows.

Mrs. Smith looked at Mr. Smith. Mr. Smith did not return her look; he just spooned ravioli into his mouth, trying not to get any sauce on his mustache.

"Come on, guys!" Mrs. Smith tried again. "You have all of summer ahead of you! Big plans! Big projects! The world is your oyster!"

"I thought I'd take up taxidermy," Anna said.

"Miss *Smith*," her mother growled. "Don't even joke."

Clark knew that Anna would probably do the same thing she did every summer. She would wear her seasonally inappropriate dark and heavy clothes and hang around with her friends who were always inappropriate, no matter what season it was. She wouldn't really *do* anything, unless she could get one of the coveted jobs at Hot Topic.

"What about you, Clark?" his mother asked.

"First I'm going to finish that Dragons of the Realm series. After that I'll try *Cursed Child* again. If you let me, I'm going to the library *every day* on my bike."

He was so excited by the imaginary stack of books waiting for him that at first he didn't notice his audience's reaction.

His mother was staring at him silently. So was his dad, but his gaze was slightly off-center.

Whoops. He *should* have said something like *learn to swim the breast stroke properly* or *teach myself chess*. But the opportunity was past.

Mrs. Smith took a deep breath.

"You guys. Come *on*. You're young! This is *summer!* You're *kids!* Don't waste it!"

"We're not wasting it," Anna drawled. "We're doing exactly what we're supposed to do. As kids. Hang out and have fun."

Mrs. Smith narrowed her eyes and bit her lip but didn't say anything. Mr. Smith kept eating his ravioli.

After TV it was time for bed. ("It's still a school night! No partying yet!") Darkness finally—and completely—overcame the yard outside. Clark brushed his teeth as fast as he could and peed, remembering to lower the seat carefully so it didn't crash. He ran a hand through his shaggy brown hair to keep it from becoming too tangled or weird by morning, forcing Mom to bring out the Brush.

In his parents' bathroom, Mrs. Smith was cleaning her own teeth for exactly two minutes with the help of a timer. She smiled at him with a foamy mouth. "G'night, Clark!"

"G'night, Mom!"

He was sort of glad she couldn't kiss him on the head and sort of wished she would. His father lay in bed already, looking at the ceiling, not doing anything. In his work clothes. The TV was on but nearly silent. It flooded the room with a fluttering of sickly blue light.

And then . . . for a moment . . . it looked like there was a dim cloud above the bed. As if his dad were smoking. But there was no smell and of course Mr. and Mrs. Smith didn't smoke. The haze swirled slowly and oozily above him.

But when Clark squinted, trying to look directly at it, the smoke wasn't there at all.

The room seemed darker and gloomier now, and all the colors looked dimmer. The silence was overwhelming.

"Good night, Dad!" Clark called out, more loudly than he really needed to.

"g'night love you," his dad said back, still staring at the ceiling.

Clark made himself continue down the dark hall. Through her open door, he could see that Anna also was lying on her bed in her day clothes—but she was on her phone, fingers flying over the screen. Actually *doing* something. Sort of.

"G'night," he said.

"G'night, squirt," she said without bothering to look up.

But there was still enough love in that to get Clark the last few feet down the hall to his own room. He turned on the light, changed into his video-game pajamas, and closed the door—leaving it open the barest crack, of course.

And then, before turning off the light again, he arranged his stuffed animals.

In the center of his bed he put his two biggest: Winkum on the right and Draco on the left. Winkum was his most beloved old horse and always held this position of honor. Draco, powerful with his fiery red felt breath and spiky tail, guarded the left side of Clark.

Next and farther out from them were Bo Bear and Pog (always together. Pog was a small bunny, lanky and old and easily transportable but not that strong) and on the other side was the relatively new Dark Horse, whose fur was still smooth and whose flanks rippled with muscle. Beyond them were FlapFish and Dynamo the Diprotodon and Gribble, and Kevin and Ducky and Raccoon and Baz.

On the outside edges were the smallest stuffed animals. Random, cheap weird creatures given to Clark by his uncle or won in a claw machine. The ones he would miss less if anything Happened.

(This was a shameful thing to admit, but it was also the truth.)

All of the animals were faced out. *Away* from where Clark

would lie in the middle, safely between Winkum and Draco. So they could watch. The closet door, the windows, the scary, cold floor he couldn't see from his pillow. Shadowed corners.

They were always on the lookout for monsters.

Once everyone was in his or her proper position, Clark turned off the light and hopped carefully into his place in the center. He would have preferred to hug Winkum *facing* him; it was more comfortable. But the horse needed to keep an eye out. So his tail tickled Clark's neck; that's just the way it was.

Then Clark said his good nights to everyone he hadn't been able to tell personally. He couldn't say this for certain, but felt that this little ritual also kept monsters away.

"Good night, Grandma and Grandpa Smith"—who were in California.

"Good night, Grandma Machen"—who was just over in Hixville.

"Good night, Grandpa Ken"—who was wherever people were when they died.

"Good night, Aaron and Nathan"—who were the cousins he never got to see.

"Good night, Shantel. Yankees rule, Sox drool!"—who was his best friend from kindergarten and had just moved to Boston.

And then, even though he *knew* they weren't real and he *knew* it was childish, he said good night to the others.

"Good night, Superman and Batman," he whispered.

Neither of them had parents to say good night to them. Maybe they missed it. Even after becoming grown-up heroes.

"Good night, Wonder Woman." (Even though she did have a mom.)

And then, *finally,* Clark was able to snuggle down between his two walls of stuffed animals, sheets and covers pulled suffocatingly overhead. He drifted off, dreaming of summer.

FOON

okay u dont see me here cuz i am not here yet. u see others but not me. i am not. yet.

TWO

Still Night

The clock said 4:37 a.m. in bright, bright red.

Clark never got up to pee and was not sure what had woken him. He quickly counted his stuffed animals, looking left and right as his eyes adjusted.

Baz. The tiny monkey.

He had been on the farthest outside, to the left.

And now he was gone.

Clark's heart began to race.

He really, *really* didn't want to stick his head back out of the blankets and pillows. But the little stuffed animal needed him.

He closed his eyes and tried to summon a teaspoon of courage. He thought of every cool and brave comic book character he had ever loved.

Then he peeped over the side of the bed and looked.

There on the floor lay Baz, simply fallen out of bed.

But . . . *was* it that simple?

He had been on the *other* side of Clark at the beginning of the night. On the part facing the wall, not the windows.

How did he wind up on the wrong side?

It wasn't possible.

At least the little guy looked all right.

But . . . was the closet door opened a crack?

That wasn't good. Clark had made sure it was closed before going to sleep, like he always did. Just like he always made sure his bedroom door was always left *open* a crack.

Didn't matter. Wasn't going to think about it. There was a rescue to be done.

Clark squirmed around, keeping as much of his body under the blankets as he could. Eventually he managed to angle himself so that only his torso stuck out over the side of the bed. His carefully ordered lineup of stuffed animals was shattered and a couple of guys were temporarily squished—but thankfully, no one else fell over the sides.

He braced his toes over the mattress edge to keep from falling to the floor himself.

With a quick swipe Clark grabbed Baz by the tail. He managed to do this without even touching the ground—or anything else. Then he threw himself back into the middle of the bed with a ninja-like roll. The bedsheets tangled around his legs like ropes. Stuffed animals flew. But none fell. Everyone, including the little monkey and Clark himself, was safe.

He held up Baz and viewed him critically.

Was one eye pulled slightly, tearing the cloth around it? Had it been that way before? Was his painted nose scratched?

Why was there dust all over him? Hairy, *big* dust? Like... like he had fallen off the bed and then been *dragged underneath it* to the other side...

Clark carefully wiped off the tiny monkey and tucked him back in, a little closer to the center this time.

But still facing out. Watching.

There was more night before morning.

THREE

Day

Morning was glorious. Last day of school! Clark's room was blasted with sunlight, yellow and warm.

He was in such a good mood he almost forgot to check his stuffed animals....

But not quite. There had been some settling and confusion, a few guys switched places. Otherwise everyone was more or less still where they were originally deployed.

In the sunlight, Baz definitely looked a little worse for the wear. The rips and dust implied incredibly creepy things. Something *had* gone after the monkey...something that pulled it under the bed and chewed. Something Clark definitely didn't want to think about, even in daylight hours. He would switch Baz out with someone else that night to give the little monkey a rest.

Breakfast was special: Mrs. Smith marked every occasion with a Meal. Today it was maple sausages and toast with little butter suns on them, their rays melting into the bread.

"Last day of school!" Mrs. Smith cried. She already wore the large earpiece that stuck out of her head all day. Her job was calling people and trying to get them to pay their credit card bills. She also was starting up her own LifestylePositivityEnhancement counseling service, which seemed to mostly involve telling people the same sort of encouraging things she told Clark and Anna every day, but for money.

Mr. Smith already had his bag, leaving for his job at the bank while Anna and Clark ate and Mrs. Smith hopped around, cleaning, organizing, packing, drinking green tea.

"havegoodday," he mumbled, and then walked into the wall.

Everyone stared at him.

He stared at the wall.

Mrs. Smith moved first, taking him by the shoulders in a sort of hug and carefully turned him toward the door.

"Honey, you okay there?"

"imfine"

She kissed him on the cheek and brushed the edges of his mustache with her fingers, getting every hair in place.

"If you say so . . . Try to have a good day, darling. Be careful driving! Don't drive *into* anything! Ha-ha!"

There was sunlight, and Mrs. Smith's cheery face.

There was Mr. Smith, slumped and ashen. *Drained.*

Clark thought about the fog above the bed from the night before. The one that wasn't there. Was it just a coincidence that it appeared and then the next morning Mr. Smith was all sickly and worn-looking?

Toast stuck to the sides of Clark's suddenly dry throat. The morning turned sour.

Mr. Smith left. Everyone in the kitchen remained tense until they heard the car pull safely out of the driveway.

"C'mon, guys!" Mrs. Smith called out, trying to break the mood. "*PIC*tures!"

They went into the backyard where the bushes were just becoming the dark green of serious summer. Birds flitted and called. Mrs. Smith got down on one knee and pulled out the *real* camera. Not her phone. Anna humphed impatiently, shifting back and forth from leg to leg under her long black skirt. She adjusted and readjusted her giant black leather bag.

Clark had put on what he knew his mother would like him to wear on the last day of school: his nicest shorts, the khaki ones with the white belt and brass buckle. A dark blue polo shirt that his mom thought made him look like someone who sailed boats. His best sneakers. He *probably* looked okay, but more importantly the outfit avoided an argument.

"*Cheese*," Clark said.

"*Organically produced tofu-based cheese product,*" Anna said.

Click!

"Oh, you guys are growing so much!!!"

Mrs. Smith let the camera dangle from her wrist, sniffed, and tried to hug them. Clark hugged back. Anna stiffened and then gave up. For such a small woman their mother was surprisingly strong. It was probably because of the weights she lifted while on her phone calls.

"We'll go to the mall after school! Get an end-of-school treat for each of you!"

"Cool," Anna said.

"Thanks!" Clark said.

Happily, brother and sister turned to go.

"*CLARK!*"

Mrs. Smith's voice had a spank in it.

Clark wilted. He had forgotten that when he turned his back she would see.

His mother pulled the stuffed animal out of his pocket. It was Kevin, a (tiny) adorable polar bear whose mouth was permanently sewn closed in a smile. Clark imagined he had fierce teeth behind the stitches.

"Clark," Mrs. Smith said again, disappointment deep in her voice.

"Bye," he said, kissing her on the cheek, which would probably silence her. He ran to catch up with his sister before his mom could say anything else.

"*Subtlety.* You gotta learn that," Anna said. She shifted her giant bag and the huge mess of charms, keys, dangles, puffballs, and glittering gewgaws attached to its strap clinked significantly.

Hidden among them were a furry plastic monkey sucking its thumb, a little goth penguin, a zombie made out of string.

They were nice, but they weren't *real* stuffed animals.

Warnock Elementary and Middle School was brick. It had nice green fields and an excellent playground. It had a flagpole with an American flag that always flew at the top except when the weather was bad or someone important had died. Inside it had shiny tiled floors, spacious classrooms, and an auditorium with deep-red velvet curtains.

Clark was very much looking forward to *never seeing it again*. Until fall.

"Hey, Clark, what stuffed animal did ya bring today?"

Ben Eldritch was a big part of the reason Clark was glad to say good-bye to Warnock.

He was taller than Clark, heavier than Clark, and all around more *solid* than Clark. He had light hair of no real color and an ugly nose. He and his two little helper friends—who were more Clark-size—surrounded him.

Clark sighed. Maybe this one time his mom was right to remove Kevin.

The boys patted him down. When no stuffed animal was found, their leader growled in disappointment.

"Check his bag," he ordered.

Clark dutifully handed over his backpack. The two boys ripped through it quickly and efficiently. Unable to come up with anything incriminating—except for a couple of questionable pencils with fuzzy Halloween bat and cat toppers—they gave up and shrugged.

"He's clean," the one on the right said.

"What did your mom pack you for lunch today?" Ben demanded.

The kid on the left obediently held out the lunch sack.

Ben pawed through it.

"Italian hero . . . homemade? Apple slices . . . *Fritos* . . . a RING DING!"

Clark sagged. His mom almost never packed them sweets for lunch. Just on special days, like this one.

"Take it," he mumbled.

"Thanks, think I will," Ben said sweetly, already opening it and shoving it into his mouth. He turned to go, tossing the bag of Fritos carelessly behind him. The two helpers fought for it with the snarls of wild pigs. "Have a great last day."

Clark sighed again, reshouldered his bag, and headed to the main office.

Miss Nugganoth sat as she always did, solidly and mostly unmoving behind her desk. As if she were stone and this was where she lived, day and night. A single finger pecked at keys on her computer.

"Good morning, Miss Nugganoth," Clark said.

"Very busy this morning, Charles. It had better be important. Can't waste my whole day with jibberjab from kids."

"Ben and those other boys bullied me again today," he reported. "They took part of my lunch."

"I'll file the official complaint as soon as I finish this other paperwork. You know my job isn't just catering to you lollygaggers and puddlewinkers. I have *administrative tasks* to complete, Charles."

"Thank you, Miss Nugganoth," Clark said politely.

He was always polite. This was the sixty-seventh time they'd had this conversation this year. Each and every time he was polite. And each time she called him a different name starting with *C*.

He told his mom about the bullying exactly twice. The second time she had gone a little crazy and called everyone: the school, the boys' parents, their reverend.

The next day Ben and his two thugs had held Clark down and given him the worst wedgie of his life.

So he stopped telling his mom.

In math he drew a picture of a monster eating Ben, head first. Then he scratched it out. Even Ben didn't deserve that fate.

He looked at the big clock above the teacher's head. Only two more hours before he was free.

At 2:30 p.m. Clark's mom was waiting for him in her bright red car. Anna was riding shotgun. Clark happily changed direction, escaping the long line that trickled like ants to the stinky yellow buses.

Even his sister was perkier than her usual self. She had a rare smile on her black-painted lips and a tiny, colorful pinwheel that spun as she held it out the window. Clark wondered where she got it. Did teachers give out toys on the last day of *high school?* Ms. Shambleau had given him another Halloween pencil with a cat on top.

"Off to the mall, kiddos!" Mrs. Smith cried merrily. "How was everything? How was your last day? Did you guys sign autograph books for each other? We used to do that. Do you have an autograph book? I should get you an autograph book. I wonder if they have autograph books at the mall.... Yes, Mrs. Patel, I'm listening...."

Clark saw the telltale turn of his mom's head, which indicated the person on her earpiece was saying something she needed to pay attention to.

"Yes, but you missed your last four payments, Mrs. Patel. We're going to have to close your account, and you don't want that, do you, Mrs. Patel?"

Clark unrolled his window and leaned against the door, watching all the summer things go by. A sign at the church advertised a CAR WASH tomorrow. Stones and plants spelled out words like GROW and SEED at the hardware store. Shiny mowers with bright red price tags filled the overflow lot.

He could *smell* summer things, too. The oily scent of hot tar. The moist heat of dark green leaves. The dry dust of what was once a puddle and would be a puddle again after the next thunderstorm.

Eventually the mall appeared like a castle on a hill, gleaming and white. In the parking lot Mrs. Smith held Clark's hand and looked like she wanted to hold Anna's.

That was not going to happen, of course.

First they went to a fancy coffee shop. Anna's eyes glittered at the drink choices. Clark made for the cookies and pastries.

"Wait—didn't I already pack a treat for you today?" Mrs. Smith asked.

Clark froze, his face and hands already pressed up against the glass that protected rows of amazing-looking sweets.

"I, uh, gave my Ring Ding to Ben." Which wasn't *exactly* a lie.

"That was so nice of you!" his mom said, kissing him on the head. "You're becoming such a generous, good little man. I'm very proud of how you turned around your relationship with that bully. Choose whatever you want! Even the big pieces of cake."

Feeling only a little guilty, Clark managed to wolf down an entire triple-chocolate napoleon with a chocolate butterfly decoration. Anna sipped some giant frozen mocha-chocolate-coffee explosion thing.

"Hey look, there's the Science-porium Edutainment Store!" Mrs. Smith said after they finished their snacks and began walking around the mall. "Clark, why don't you choose something from there?"

He examined the telescopes. Telescopes were neat; you could look at the moon with them. There were Icky Science Kits, which you could make slime with. There were butterfly nets and ant farms and microscopes you could connect to your computer.

And then Clark saw it.

The giant pile of Incredibly Realistic Yet Unbelievably Squishy Zoological Specimens. The display must have been six feet tall and ten feet wide at the base—extremely tempting to take a running leap into.

On the very top of that giant pile of Specimens was an unimaginably magnificent snowy owl. Her fur was so white it practically glowed. She had a fluffy royal mantle of fake feathers around her neck and glass eyes that shone like jewels. Her wings were correctly shaped and her feet had realistically hard talons under downy-soft fuzz.

In short, she was the most beautiful and regal stuffed animal Clark had ever seen.

"...Really?" his mom said, seeing what he was looking at. She bit the straw in her drink.

"You said." Clark stuck his lower lip out. "*Anything.* I could choose."

"Yeah, but..." His mom looked around desperately. "Look at that Dark Matter Monopoly! Doesn't that look like fun? The...uh...Community Chest lights up when a...neutrino hits it! Or something."

Clark just stood there. His mom could deal with a lot of things, but silence wasn't one of them.

"Oh, all *right*," she said, sighing.

He could feel her disappointment like rain on his head. But he didn't care.

Much.

At Hot Topic Mrs. Smith just looked defeated when Anna showed her what *she* wanted. It was an old-timey bathing suit with long shorts and a sort of T-shirt top, all black, with lace and little red skull buttons.

Mrs. Smith was quiet on the trip home. She was probably wondering what she had done wrong to produce two such weird kids. Anna was gleefully texting everyone she knew about her new bathing suit. Clark was reading the booklet that came with Snowy.

Snowy owls like to eat lemmings but can hunt creatures as big as ducks and as slippery as fish. The males are often pure white. Both parents care for the babies.

That night Clark carefully laid Snowy in a position of honor, on his right. Still farther out from Winkum, of course. He stroked her furry mantle, said his good nights to everyone, and went to sleep happily waiting for the next day to come.

FOON

that big white bird a good 1. strong. full of powers. good warrior. even on furst night, when new, furst time awake.

shes the only reason baz made it thru that night

FOUR

Night

Clark woke with his heart beating too loudly.

He grabbed the first stuffed animal he saw—Snowy—and clutched her to his chest.

There was absolute silence.

As his eyes adjusted, shadows writhed and squirmed on the ceiling.

Clark blinked. It had to be a trick of the light. Shadows couldn't move by themselves. Especially if there were no objects—or light—to make those shadows to begin with.

His feet were freezing despite the fact that all his covers were still on. He counted his stuffed animals.

Two were missing.

Baz and *Gribble* this time, the lizard monster thing from the old cartoon.

Clark moved, very slowly, to look over the side of his bed.

They lay on the floor, their feet in the air.

Out of reach.

Clark's stomach sank into his icy feet.

There was no way he was going to get out of bed. There was no way he was going to set a single toe on the cold, deadly floor.

They would have to stay there until morning.

What could he do to help them?

Feeling sick, he realized the answer was in his hands. *Snowy.* She was big and powerful and could protect the two little stuffed animals.

Clark closed his eyes and pretended he hadn't thought of the idea.

Nope.

There was no turning back. It really was the only answer.

With reluctance and regret, Clark carefully tossed Snowy so she landed right next to Baz and Gribble.

He huddled back down under the covers, whispering, "Sorry."

He stayed there, awake, a long time before sleep finally came.

FIVE

Day

Clark opened his eyes woozily. It was *late*. No alarm to wake him up—no tickly fingers of his mom to wake him up, either. The events of the night before seemed fuzzy. It was a few minutes before he remembered the scary shadows and Baz and Gribble and Snowy on the floor.

He scrambled out of bed to grab them up and cuddle them—but only Baz and Snowy were there.

"You did your best," he whispered to the owl. "It was your first night. You tried really hard. Thank you."

Then he put them back on the pillows, Baz tucked under the owl's pale wing and up against Winkum's chest. The little monkey could use some extra comfort.

Then Clark looked under his bed.

No Gribble.

He looked under the radiators.

Still no Gribble.

He looked everywhere—even the closet, now harmless in daylight.

No Gribble.

Clark swallowed, feeling sick.

He would find him. Where could the little lizard possibly have gone?

He took a deep breath—a deep *cleansing* breath, his mother would say—and padded down the hall. Anna was still asleep, of course. Mr. Smith had already left. Mrs. Smith was downstairs somewhere, working.

On a whim, Clark looked under his parents' bed.

Gribble!

Clark scooped him up and hugged him tight and then gave him a thorough examination. The lizard's lower jaw looked gnawed on. As if something like a dog had pulled him under the bed to secretly chew.

Clark felt nauseated, yet relieved. At least Gribble was safe now. He petted the little lizard and whispered to him, taking him downstairs to breakfast.

Mrs. Smith was already on the phone and there was a Nutritious Muffin on his plate. Sunflower seeds and craisins made a face on the top that smiled at him. He nibbled it, feeling a little better.

Two hours later he lay in the warm sunshine. Winkum, Draco, Black Horse, Snowy, and several of his Star Wars action figures were posed in the grass nearby (Gribble was recuperating back upstairs on his pillow, surrounded by friends). They were getting ready for the Battle for Big Rock while Clark took a little lie-down nearby. He was reading *The Return of the King*, which was hard going but had a lot of battle strategy in it. He needed to up his game against the monsters if he was going to make sure that he *and* all his stuffed animals survived the nights.

Anna sprawled on a lawn chair nearby. She held her little black parasol perfectly upright in one hand, her latest historical fiction novel in the other. Giant curlicue black sunglasses covered her face like a bug.

Between the brother and sister was a plate of slowly diminishing iced lemon cookies.

Everything was awesome.

Then a shadow passed between him and the sun. The world darkened.

Clark lowered his book.

His mom was standing there, grinning. Her hands were on her hips.

This was a bad sign. This was the sign of A Decision.

A decision, Clark knew, that would perfectly screw up his perfect first day of summer vacation.

"Clark! You'll never believe it! I got you a *playdate!*"

Clark cautiously raised an eyebrow. In theory, this could be a good thing. Playdates *could* be fun. He hadn't had one in a long time.

"There's this woman I met, Lisa Lee. She has a son going into fifth grade next year, too. At St. Luke's. His name is Derleth."

Clark waited.

"You'll like him. He's really fun. He's into baseball, video games, all sorts of sports...."

Anna snorted. Even *she* could see where this was going.

"I think you could learn a lot from him. He's a really good kid. Just...you know. A good, normal kid. Maybe he can show you stuff. Baseball cards. How to throw a ball."

Annnnnd there it was. The *angle*. His mom had arranged a playdate with what she thought was a normal kid, hoping that some of his normal-ness would rub off on Clark. He tried not to let the disappointment ooze out his pores and melt down his face like lemon icing in the sunlight.

"He'll be over here at eleven."

And there went his perfect summer day and war plans, ruined.

Clark waited for the boy with a face rewashed by him, hair rebrushed by his mom. He felt shiny and dry in the cool living room. Outside the sun was still glowing madly. Anna had disappeared; something about trying to find the kiddie pool that was in the garage so she could try out her new bathing suit.

At 11:01 a new red minivan like something out of an ad

poured itself off the road and up their driveway. Clark's mom opened the front door and another mom stood there, wearing a baseball cap that matched her son's.

"HI, KIM!"

"HI, LISA!"

"THIS IS MY SON, DERLETH! DERLETH AUGUST! HIS FRIENDS CALL HIM D. A.!"

"THIS IS CLARK!"

"SO NICE TO MEET YOU, CLARK. WE SHOULD HAVE DONE THIS AGES AGO!"

"IT'S SO TRUE!"

The two moms chatted loudly for a while and then the one said good-bye and the other ruffled Clark's hair and said she was going to make lunch and hoped everyone liked pasta salad and then she left, too.

Clark and the boy stood there uncertainly.

The boy was almost exactly like Ben Eldritch.

He was bigger than Clark, more *solid* than Clark, maybe even bigger than Ben. His hair was dark but definitely no particular color under his cap. He held a glove and ball and bat all at the same time. With no difficulty. He did shift a little on his feet. But that seemed to be more from the uncomfortable silence they were both experiencing than an inability to carry a bunch of things—and himself—at the same time.

"Your house smells funny," D. A. finally said.

"Doesn't everyone's house smell funny to other people?" Clark asked.

"Yeah, I guess. But yours smells *funny* funny."

Clark couldn't smell anything. But... taking a look around... he had to admit that it didn't seem like a particularly *friendly* house. All of the downstairs lights were off to conserve energy. The air conditioner was in its off cycle—also to conserve energy—and everything was quieter than usual. Nothing stirred, and they had no pets. Everything seemed... dead.

"Hey, show me your room," D. A. suggested.

"Okay," Clark said, relieved.

As they went up the stairs he was surprised to see the other boy go slowly, pausing at the same steps Clark did every night. The ones that creaked.

That was strange.

Clark always thought—because his parents always told him—that he was a scaredy-cat and most kids his age weren't afraid of things that squeaked when they shouldn't.

As they passed by his parents' darkened bedroom, Clark could have sworn the other boy shuddered.

But he brightened the moment they got to Clark's room.

He actually grinned when he saw the bed and the pile of stuffed animals.

"Oh, thank *goodness!*" D. A. said, making a beeline for them—not the models, or Star Wars toys, or Legos. He put his sports stuff down on the floor so he had both hands free and waggled his fingers with expectation. "I was so worried. Your house is *dark*, man."

"What?"

None of the other boy's words or behavior made sense. Now he was systematically picking up each stuffed animal and turning it over. Clark rushed to intervene, waiting for the inevitable scorn and then threat to his possessions.

But... unlike Ben, this boy was handling each guy carefully, and really, *really* looking at it. Closely. Like he was examining or reviewing it.

"Your house. It's all dark and gross and creepy and weird," D. A. said offhandedly. "Totally haunted by a Monster of some kind. It's good you've got protection."

"What?" Clark asked again.

"*Protection*, dummy," D. A. said, but not meanly. "Against the Monsters. You've got the beginnings of a really nice army here."

Clark blinked. Did he just say Monsters? Out loud, for real?

D. A. frowned at his expression.

"Has no one ever told you...?"

"*What?* Told me what?"

"I don't get it," D. A. said, confused. "You obviously know *something*, because of all these guys here."

"I sleep with them all. Every night," Clark said slowly. Was he really telling D. A. this? This secret about himself? "I turn them face out. So they can... They'll see... I don't know. Monsters. Like you said."

"*Right,*" D. A. said triumphantly. "Of course you do! You get it. So I don't have to tell you that Monsters are evil and terrible and will try to eat you or drain your life essence, right?"

"No. I mean yes. I mean—really? This is all true?"

"Uh-huh, for sure." D. A. nodded sagely. "You know it. C'mon. I guess no one told you, but...you *feel* it."

"Mom and Dad say that's just..."

"Grown-ups don't know about Monsters anymore and can't get hurt by them," D. A. interrupted impatiently. As if this were something that was so obvious it didn't even need to be discussed. "So you can't get hurt if you're asleep with adults in the room. But none of us sleep with our parents anymore, which is why we need the Stuffies."

"Stuffies?"

"Stuffed *animals*, bro!" D. A. whacked him playfully on the shoulder. "Keep up! The Stuffies protect us from the Monsters. The Monsters try to get us. There are all sorts of Monsters, and you can't build any room that will keep them all out. Some are, you know, really skinny, some can float through the air, some can squish themselves down to nothing. Some look kind of like bugs. They get in the cracks when there's no door or closet or space under the bed or whatnot."

"Wait. You've *seen* them? Really? Monsters?"

"I mean, no, but I know people who know this stuff. Legit, for real."

It was too much to take in at once. Everything Clark ever secretly believed about Monsters coming to get him was all *real*?

D. A. continued blithely on, unaware of the dazed look on Clark's face.

"Yeah, and supposedly some rituals keep them away, but no one knows any really powerful ones. And they only work for a little while. No, the only really good protection is a solid army of Stuffies. You're a little undisciplined here, and you might need to do some better resource allocation of your troops, but you're on the right track. Take this guy here, he's a tank."

He shook Draco, but not too hard.

"A tank?"

"Yeah. A tank. A bruiser. A fighter. Strong soldier. You know. He's big, so that's, like, a plus one, and he's got fangs and horns, and so that's another plus two. Add that to a base of three, and you've got at least an MPF of six here."

"MPF?"

"Monster Protection Factor. Listen up, this is super important. You start with a base of three for most guys. Then you add plus one for each additional attack feature ... fangs, horns, claws, stuff like that. You get one point for size, if it's big. You minus one if it's small, like beanbag–size. Like this guy, he's a two."

He picked up Kevin to illustrate.

Clark felt weirdly defensive on behalf of his little polar bear. "I always imagined he has sharp teeth, just that he can't always show them...."

"That's okay," D. A. said soothingly. "*Sustainably imagined* things count. That means things you've always thought were there but you can't see, but you didn't just make up on the spot. Those are worth half a point. So he's got an MPF of two and a half."

"A Monster Protection Factor of two and a half," Clark repeated slowly, looking at Kevin as if for the first time.

"And this guy here." D. A. picked up Winkum.

Clark almost lunged forward to stop the boy from touching his most beloved stuffed animal but forced himself not to.

"He *looks* like a three—medium-size, just a horse, no real attack features. *But* he's obviously loved. And old. He's your favorite, right?"

Clark nodded reluctantly.

"So he gets a plus two. Love gives you special powers. He's a five. Whoa—look at this guy. He's the *bomb*. Just look at him," D. A. said, picking up Snowy.

"Her. I got her yesterday," Clark said proudly.

"She's *fierce*. Look at those claws. C'mon, let's add these guys all up properly."

Still a little bewildered, Clark found a piece of paper and pen and took notes and did the math as the other boy went through all of his stuffed animals. Sometimes he had to explain the animal's background or the special abilities he or she or it had.

D. A. peppered his math with stories about his own collection. "I'm more of an action-figure guy myself," he admitted. "I got hundreds of them. But they're just like barely half a quarter point each. Cannon fodder. But when you add 'em all up you get *insane* Defense. I set 'em up around my bed on the floor every night and my parents think I'm doing these big war games. I am, sorta," he added thoughtfully. "No Monster got me yet."

"How do you know when a Monster...gets you?" Clark asked timidly.

"Oh, you *know*," the other boy said darkly. "They don't get you all at once. Usually. They take little bits of you. Of like

37

your spirit or soul or whatever. They empty you out. You stop feeling. You get tired all the time and pale. You don't feel like doing anything. Like a vampire's eating you, or something? And then, eventually, when you're weak enough... *MUNCH*."

Clark jumped.

His dad was pale and lifeless and confused. And there were those strange shadows that seemed to drift around his head like smoke....

"What do Monsters look like, exactly?"

"I dunno, like, details and stuff. We're not supposed to be able to see them. Only *they* can." He pointed at the stuffed animals.

"But... I *thought* I saw one. Or something. Hovering around my dad."

"Your *dad?*" D. A. asked, horrified. "Grown-ups are supposed to be totally safe."

"He's been acting really weird. Like you said, all slow and... weird. Confused."

"I don't know. Maybe he just has low iron. My mom takes supplements. Although"—D. A. cocked his head, considering—"your parents' bedroom was kind of... terrifying."

"It's not..." Clark started to say. Then he realized that the only time he went in there was to say good night or when they called him in, and then it was only reluctantly. He usually hovered by the threshold. And Gribble had been taken in there by *something*.... "Okay, it *is* pretty creepy. But do you know anyone it's happened to? Like, someone who's actually been attacked by a Monster?"

"My cousin knew this girl. She...just kind of faded away. Weaker and weaker. And one day she didn't show up for school. Monster lunch. I am *totally* not letting that happen to me. Or anyone I like," he added, sticking his chin out.

"How come you know all this?" And how come I don't? Clark wanted to add.

"My cousin told me. Same cousin who knew the girl. Also my brother. Some of it you just sort of work out, when you see who gets through the night and who, uh, *doesn't*." He indicated the Stuffies with a tip of his head, as if he didn't want them to hear.

Clark thought about Gribble. "I almost lost someone last night. He's okay, but it was really scary."

"Oh man, that's the worst," D. A. said sympathetically. "But if it happens again, don't give up immediately. It takes a *lot* to drag things to the Other Side. Look around all the really scary places in your house. In the day," he added quickly, seeing the look on Clark's face. "Like, in the basement, or attic, or under your parents' bed...The really quiet places. You know, go around your house and really *listen*. When it feels like nothing, and it's like a *bad* nothing, look there."

That was exactly right, Clark realized. It was the feeling when you suddenly find yourself alone in your own house, and even though there is someone maybe two rooms over, you feel like they are a million miles away. And something very bad, and very scary, could happen at any second.

"My friend Catherine-Lucille told me that part," D. A. said. "About the listening. She's...uh...intense. But real smart. I made her one of these."

He picked up his backpack and turned it around so Clark could see the zipper. Dangling from it was a tiny felt monster. Or maybe a zombie. It was carefully sewn with big stitches around the outside and had stitch claws and bead eyes. Its tiny black thread mouth was crammed with even tinier white thread teeth.

"You *made* this?" Clark asked in awe.

"Yeah," D. A. said, a little proudly. A *little* defensively. "Like I said, I'm more of an action-figure guy, but they don't have the fight of real Stuffies. And handmade ones are the most powerful. They get an automatic plus two. So even with this guy's tiny size he's two and a quarter. Plus I put a stone that I found at the beach inside of him....I don't know, but I kind of feel like having something real in there for a heart, that you like, it helps somehow. No one's told me about a rule for that. Sometimes you just get a feeling about things. Trust your gut, like my dad says.

"Anyway, you should totally learn how to make these guys. When you give them to people they sort of *have* to put it on their bags or purses or phones or whatever. You can guilt them into it because you made it for them. So they're always a little protected. Like your friends who think it's all dumb and pretend not to believe in any of it."

Protected. Could Clark somehow make his dad carry one?

The two boys spent the rest of the afternoon indoors and out, trying different scenarios and new troop configurations with Clark's stuffed animals. There were places he hadn't even thought to put them—because they weren't in the bed. Which was where Stuffies belonged, he thought. But D. A. said one had to stand watch in front of the closet, and he would need additional troops in front of the window.

Also it didn't hurt to have extra Stuffies set out around the room randomly, ready to outflank any Monsters that managed to make their way through, *before* they could reach the bed.

All throughout his lectures and drills D. A. politely asked Clark how each stuffed animal sounded when it talked, and if there were any habits or special abilities of the Stuffy that weren't immediately obvious.

In short, it was hands down, without question, no-holds-barred, the best playdate ever.

But Clark could *feel* his mom hovering in the shadows of the hall a long time before she announced that lunch was ready. *Watching.* He could sense her disappointment that such a sporty, normal-seeming kid played so happily with Clark's stuffed animals.

This was not *her* idea of the best playdate ever.

If he wanted more playdates with his new best friend D. A., he'd better make sure they spent some time throwing the baseball around in the backyard—where she could see.

D. A.'s Amazing Zipper Dangle How-To!

Warning, guys: it's reeealllly hard to come up with a dangle Stuffy who totals more than a 2.5. You can give 'em all the claws and fangs you want, but they're just too tiny to do much, like action figures. Think of them as super emergency backup charms.

What you need:

STUFFY SKIN (cloth)
Felt is best and easiest, but whatever you have to work with.

NEEDLE

THREAD
Whatever you got. In a pinch, dental floss works.

SCISSORS

STUFFY STUFFING
Fiber fill *or* Cotton balls (pulled apart and made fluffy) *or* Crumpled-up-other-cloth

IMAGINATION!
Yeah, I know how that sounds. But seriously. You need more imagination than skill to make the most powerful Stuffies.

Optional but helpful:

TAPE
For holding the cloth together, or your pattern to the cloth.

GLUE
Fabric glue is best, superglue second-best, but almost anything will work except for glue sticks.

EYES

Googly eyes, buttons, beads, pieces of cloth cut into tiny circles.

HEART

Whatever is small but you feel would make the Stuffy real.

OTHER COLORED THREAD and/or CLOTH, PENS, FABRIC or ACRYLIC PAINT

For details.

READ THROUGH ALL THE INSTRUCTIONS FIRST!

Step 1
Drawing and outting the Stuffy's shape out of cloth

If you come up with your own design, don't start out making it too detailed or it might be hard to cut and sew. Think balloons, doughnuts, clouds, fat teddy bears, and other puffy things.

If you want to use a shape you find on the internet or elsewhere (once you have your parent or guardian's permission, of course), you can transfer it to your cloth using one of the following methods:

1. Do it by eye (look at it and then draw it freehand on the *WRONG SIDE* of the cloth. The wrong side is the back of the cloth, usually plain, unpatterned, or a lighter color).

2. If the cloth is thin or light colored, put the pattern flat on a computer screen, bright window, or electronic tablet, and put the cloth on top, *WRONG SIDE UP,*

so you can see your design through it. Trace around the shape. DO NOT DRAW ON THE SCREEN OR WINDOW ITSELF.

3. Copy—or scan and print out—the pattern onto paper. Cut it out, place it on the *WRONG SIDE* of the cloth, trace around it. If the paper slips around on the cloth use a piece of double-sided tape to hold it down, or a couple of supertiny pieces of regular tape (you can cut right through them, and sew through them if you forget to remove the tape). Or you could go old school and use a pin through the middle of the paper and the cloth.
4. Fold the cloth in half. Make sure there is enough cloth in both layers so when you cut out the shape you just drew or traced, you get two complete shapes.
5. Cut out the shape through both layers. You should have two mirror-image shapes.

Step 2
Sewing your Stuffy, or: Welcome to the whipstitch!

Thread your needle:

- Cut a fresh end off the thread with scissors, at an angle if you can.
- Hold the thread in your left hand if you're a righty (hold it in your right hand if you're a lefty).
- Pinch the tiniest end of thread between your thumb and index finger, so just a millimeter or two of thread sticks out!
- Holding the needle in your right hand (or left, if you're a lefty), *move the needle onto the thread*, not the other way around. It's easier, trust me!

Make sure there is no more than two feet of thread total, one foot on either side of the needle's eye. Taking both ends of the thread together, tie an overhand knot or square knot with it. Or any knot, really. Just make sure there is a small lumpy ball at the end of your thread so the thread won't pull through the cloth.

With such a small Stuffy, you don't really need to pin the two pieces of cloth together (or tape them or whatever), unless you really feel you need to. Just use your left hand and pinch the two pieces of cloth together in the center as you sew with your right (all opposite, of course, if you're a lefty!).

The whipstitch:

- Push the needle through from whichever side you decide is the "back" of your Stuffy to its "front." Make it about a millimeter from the edge of the cloth. Pull snugly until the knot pulls against the cloth in the back.

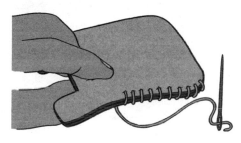

- Repeat repeatedly.
- In other words: Just keep pushing the needle through the two layers of cloth from the back, about two millimeters to the left of the previous stitch and a millimeter from the edge. Pull snugly each time, but not so tightly the cloth bunches up. ALSO, KEEP TRACK of all your thread loops and ends. If you wind up putting your needle both through the cloth and the thread loop, you will have made a blanket stitch. Which is fine, but it won't match the other stitches.
- Keep doing this until you're about a centimeter or two from where you started.

Step 3
Stuffing your Stuffy!

Use a blunt pencil or ballpoint pen to push the filling into the tricky bits. DO NOT PUSH TOO HARD.

Do not use too much stuffing.

Step 4
Finish sewing your stuffy

Continue sewing. When you get back about to where you started, push the needle *to the back from the front*, so you wind up with the thread on the back of the stuffy.

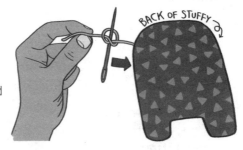

Tie a knot close to the cloth.

Hint: Tie a loose overhand knot, but then stick a needle or pin halfway through the thread loop, and pull the knot a little tightly around the pin.

Then, pulling lightly on the free end of the thread with one hand, move the pin with your other hand down the thread to the cloth, dragging the knot tied around it with it. You should be able to get the knot right up close to the cloth this way! Then pull the needle or pin out and finish pulling the knot tight.

Step 5
Sew on the dangle loop

Cut out a tiny rectangle of cloth (a snippet of ribbon is perfect for this!). When it is folded in half it should be big enough to thread a chain, wire, or cord through. Half a centimeter wide by two centimeters long should be fine.

Position the strip so one short edge is on the top front of the Stuffy's head, the loop is straight up from the Stuffy's head, and the other short edge is just on the back of the Stuffy's head. In other words, like the loop is an alligator chomping down on the tippy-top of your Stuffy's head. The front mouth bits of the alligator (the short edges of the strip) should reach just beyond the stitches holding together the top of your Stuffy's head.

Thread and knot your needle as explained before.

Insert your needle from the back through *all four layers* of cloth: the folded dangle loops and two layers of Stuffy skin sandwiched between them.

Go back down through all the layers and out the back.

Keep doing this up and down all the way across the bottom of the loop.

When you feel there's enough stitches to hold the dangle firmly, knot and cut the thread.

Step 6
Detail time!

This is the fun part. You can use pens to draw on the face, stomach, claws, horns, whatever. You can sew on bead eyes. You can cut out little tiny triangles of cloth and glue on teeth! Glue on googly eyes! Sew or glue on a different-colored belly! Attach a little teeny, tiny fancy toothpick with the frilly plastic bit on top, for a weapon!

Step 7
Hang your guy!

If you have a ball chain with a clasp, or you or your parents have an unused key ring (an ugly one no one wants to use but can't seem to throw out), that's great! If not, you can use a zip tie, string, wire, or anything else that will fit through the zipper pull and be knotted or wrapped or pulled supertight. Use a drop of superglue on any knots or slides to be extra safe.

SIX

Night

It was one thing to crawl into bed at night afraid of Monsters you weren't *quite* sure were real. It was another thing entirely to go to bed having been told by someone else that Monsters were, in fact, absolutely, positively, *dead certain*, for real.

Clark stood longer than usual at his parents' door, trying very hard to see the thing he had spotted before floating over his dad's head. Mr. Smith hadn't even made it to dinner that night, saying he was too exhausted.

Things which could have been dust or shadows, or floaters in Clark's eyes, or *anything* else at all, hung smokily at the very edges of his vision. But when he tried to focus on them, nothing was there.

"Good night, Dad," he said.

"gnightclark"

Clark wondered: *He* had stuffed animals to protect him. What did his dad have? His mom?

But why wasn't this Monster scared away by grown-ups, like it was supposed to be? D. A. said that was the first truth about Monsters, before all the other rules. You were frightened of them; they were frightened of your parents. You wanted your mom to come into your room so Monsters couldn't. You ran downstairs in the middle of the night to interrupt adult TV time because grown-ups were there. It was safe.

What other rules did the Monsters break sometimes? Clark had a thousand questions about them and the world of *Stuffies*, as his new friend called them. He wished he had gotten D. A.'s phone number or e-mail address.

He was a little worried about the future of their friendship.

His mom was on the phone with the other boy's mom as she bustled around getting ready for bed.

"I didn't know.... I didn't think it was a problem with your boy, too.... You're also concerned? It's so *amazing* to hear you say that.... We need to do something. Do you think it's good for them to hang out, or does it reinforce these behaviors? *Good night, Clark,*" she added pointedly, having noticed him standing there. She kissed him on the head and pushed him out of the room, closing the door firmly behind.

Clark put his head up against the door but couldn't hear anything distinctly.

When he passed Anna's room he caught her sneaking out

the window. Because of her complicated dress with all its nets and dangles she was struggling a little.

"Whatcha doing?" he asked.

"There's a full moon tonight. I'm going to go look." She waggled an antique-looking, not very useful-seeming brass telescope in her hand. Clark wondered where she got it.

"You could just go into the front yard. Or ask Mom and Dad," he pointed out.

Anna shrugged and carefully lowered herself out the other side.

"I like your new friend," she called from below.

Clark went to his room, now worried that Anna wouldn't be home when he went to sleep. She and her room were solid—a barrier against the darkness and Monsters. The wall they shared was safe.

Remembering the things D. A. had taught him, Clark took more care than usual in arranging his guys. Snowy went at the foot of his bed, propped up to look out into the blackness of the room. The smaller Stuffies were deployed in a semicircle around his feet. The heavy-hitters and Winkum stayed in their usual places.

Then he said his good nights to people real and imagined, and tried to sleep.

His mind whirled with worry and questions.

He was awake long after the few movements in his parents' room died down and the TV was turned off.

FOON

okays it looks like nuffing happens on this night. im reeding with you and i see you ask y? but it is what is called a _lull_. tackticks by smart other boy worked. Monsters kept away on this night.

Witch is good cuz monster getting ready to lay eggs in small Stuffy

SEVEN

Day

Perfect summer, take two.

Clark was in the backyard, having a quiet discussion with his stuffed animals about maybe acquiring some army men. Or stormtroopers. They all sat comfortably on a sheet he had spread out in the shade and listened attentively as he listed the pros and cons and read aloud from a book. It was one his uncle had given him for his fifth birthday about Roman legions, which was too long and boring for him at the time. Now he read and analyzed it intently.

Anna dozed on the lawn chair, looking a little worse for wear from her nighttime shenanigans. Clark suspected it didn't *just* involve looking at the moon. But Anna never did anything really bad beyond talking back, so he couldn't guess what it was. He studied her for a minute, thinking. Her eyes didn't flutter, so she wasn't dreaming.

"Hey, Anna?"

"Hmmph," she said, annoyed but not *that* annoyed. He was right: She hadn't been asleep.

"What's going on with Dad?"

Anna's eyes shot open like a vampire newly wakened from the dead.

"Uh," she said.

"Well," she said.

"I think it's like this," she finally said, sighing. "I think he's depressed. Or something. Or sad. Or has . . . something bad going on inside him."

Clark thought about that. He never saw their dad cry.

"Do you . . . do you think it could be a Monster?" he asked reluctantly. But he had to know.

"Like, sucking his life-force away?" Anna asked with a gentle smile.

"Yeah! Exactly!"

"That would be *amazing*. But no. I think it's some boring, old, real-world emotional garbage."

"But you said—you used to tell me when I was afraid of the night that my stuffed animals would protect me from Monsters."

"But . . . that's . . . different."

She had a funny look on her face. It wasn't exactly like she was embarrassed *now* because she had been lying to him *then*. It was more like she was remembering what she had said *then*, and somehow it didn't make sense *now*.

"Monsters scare little kids. They don't... They can't hurt adults. Everyone knows that."

Everyone knows that. Just like D. A. said. So obvious it didn't need stating.

"But if it *were* a Monster, we could kill it."

Anna opened her mouth and closed it once or twice. "Sure. That would be great. If it were a monster. We could totally take it out. But it's not, and only our dolls and stuffed animals could do that anyway."

She reached out and fluffed his hair, but Clark didn't like the pitying look on her face. She just didn't understand.

Something must have happened somewhere between age nine and sixteen that caused her to forget. That caused *everyone* to forget, eventually. Clark wondered what she saw when she looked at their dad lying there, the shadows over his face.

"Hey, *guys!*"

Their mother came out with—*not* a plate of iced lemon cookies. Instead, this time it was a plate of icy-cold vegetable slices and some sort of dip that was not creamy. Anna made a grumping noise but scooped up a handful of snap peas. Clark doubtfully took a carrot stick and stuck its tiniest end into the oily yellow stuff.

"Clark, after lunch you're going to the doctor," Mrs. Smith said crisply. Clark wilted. How many different ways were there to destroy a perfect summer day?

"Am I going to get a shot?"

"It's not that kind of doctor."

Anna looked up sharply. "Mom—"

"I can drop you off downtown." Mrs. Smith cut her daughter off without looking at her. "And we'll have a treat with Grandma after."

"Grandma!" Clark said happily.

"Bribery," Anna muttered, but she didn't refuse to go.

They went after lunch, so at least Clark had the morning to play and read. The ride was silent and tense. Anna kept sneaking looks at her brother as if she were guilty of something. Before she slid out of the car she whispered: "Don't talk about your dreams."

"Put that stupid thing away!" Mrs. Smith snapped, trying to snatch the black velvet parasol out of Anna's hands.

Despite her usual lassitude, Anna deftly avoided her mother's clutches and snapped it open with a triumphant flourish. She popped on her sunglasses and swayed down the sidewalk, elegant and monochrome. Almost beautiful.

The doctor's office was not in a hospital or medical complex; it was in a large and pretty Victorian house with white trim that Clark knew Anna would love.

Inside there was nothing on any of the walls about health or teeth or diet or how TV can kill your brain. Just little paintings of flowers and landscapes. Soft music played from somewhere unseen. Everything was carpeted and nothing was shiny. The waiting room looked like a living room with big dark couches and lots of magazines. But no TV.

The doctor stuck his head out of his office just as Mrs. Smith was poised to knock.

"Welcome."

He was an old man with crazy hair that flew around his head like a flock of untidy white birds. Gigantic black-rimmed glasses sat on his face like a mask. A loose blue cardigan hung around him, more like a cape than a sweater. Clark very, very much hoped he was a wizard.

His mother, however, did not look happy with his appearance.

"You must be Clark," the doctor said with a smile. "Mrs. Smith."

Clark's mom opened her mouth to talk.

"I'm concerned that—"

The doctor held up his hand. "Nothing now, Mrs. Smith! Let Clark and me just have our little talk, all right? I'll call you in for a consult after. It will be about forty-five minutes. Thank you."

Mrs. Smith didn't like *that* either.

Clark meekly went through the door when the doctor beckoned and felt weird when it closed behind him. He chose a big, comfy-looking leather chair and sat back in it. His feet didn't touch the floor.

"Clark, I'm Dr. Randolph Carter." The doctor threw himself into a normal office chair across from Clark. He held a clipboard and a pen. "Your mom—er, your *parents* are concerned that you're obsessed with stuffed animals. That you have too many of them."

"I have way less than Shantel!" Clark protested, leaning forward in his chair. "She has, like, a *hundred* of them! They're all over her bed and in a special hammock just for them in the corner!"

"And you're upset that because she's a girl she gets to keep more?" the doctor asked, nodding seriously.

"No, I'm just upset because she *gets* to have more. And her mom never makes a big deal out of it. My mom always does."

"Do you have a stuffed animal on you right now?"

Clark froze.

The doctor raised his bushy eyebrows, waiting.

Reluctantly Clark pulled Kevin out of his back pocket and handed him over. The doctor took the polar bear and turned it in his hands, looking at it silently. Almost like D. A. had. Then he handed Kevin back.

"Do you *always* carry a stuffed animal with you?"

"I try to," Clark admitted. He looked down at the floor. He really had to make himself a zip-pull monster like D. A.'s. That would make everything easier.

"Would it be easier if you talked to a *puppet?*"

Clark looked up: The doctor had a brightly colored, vaguely human puppet on his left hand and was waggling his fingers to make its arms flop.

"*Hi, Clark!*" the doctor said in a high voice, trying to keep his mouth closed. "*I'm Ippy!*"

Clark pushed himself back into his chair as far as he could go.

"No. I don't want to talk to the puppet."

"Don't you like puppets?" He—the doctor—looked genuinely confused. "Aren't they like stuffed animals?"

"No. It's weird. Please stop," Clark asked politely.

"Oh. All right." The doctor lowered his hand, obviously disappointed. With his other hand he scribbled something down on the clipboard. "Do you talk to your stuffed animals, Clark?"

"Yeah," Clark said, blushing.

"And...do they talk back?"

"Yeah. Sorta."

The doctor nodded heavily and wrote something strongly, with great portentousness, on the clipboard.

"And you...hear them? Like, in your ears? Outside of your head?"

"What? No!" Clark corrected quickly, seeing where the doctor was going. "I just...you know...*pretend* they talk back."

The doctor looked both relieved and (again) disappointed. He carefully crossed out whatever it was he just wrote.

But it felt like a betrayal to use the word "pretend."

There was *one* time....

It was years ago. Clark didn't think about it too much because he didn't want to wear out the memory. He was still in his little-boy bed. The morning sun was shining through his windows, and he woke up slowly, enjoying the warmth of the rays on his face. Winkum was tucked next to his head on the pillow. He had all his fur back then, and shiny eyes.

"I love you," Clark whispered.

"I love you, too," Winkum had said back.

Clark had blinked, but there was no indication the stuffed animal had ever moved. There was no proof any of it had happened. But in the magic of the sparkling morning sunlight it all seemed very possible. It all seemed very *right*. Clark had hugged Winkum tightly.

It hadn't happened since.

Clark decided not to share this with the doctor. He had only told one person, once—Ben Eldritch, who hadn't seemed so cruel at first. But he made fun of Clark and immediately told everyone in the class.

The doctor cleared his throat. He still hadn't taken the puppet off his left hand. Clark wished he would.

"Your mom says that you arrange your stuffed animals in . . . 'specific' and 'particular' positions before you go to bed."

Clark was outraged. When did his mom see that? She never came in to kiss him good night anymore. Did she sneak into his room when he was asleep?

"They're . . . I arrange them so . . . they . . ." He faltered. "They're ready if Monsters attack."

"*Ohhhhhh.*"

The doctor nodded as if everything made sense now. He sighed in relief.

"Right. Monsters. I get it. Wow. You have *no idea* how lucky you are you got me. And not someone else."

"Because you believe in Monsters?" Clark asked hopefully.

"No," he said with a chuckle. He finally took the puppet off his hand. "There are no such thing as monsters, Clark. And there's nothing wrong with you. Almost everyone is afraid of the dark when they're your age. I *still* don't like going into the garage at night without all the lights on and a big flashlight just in case."

How disappointing. If life were a fantasy book, this would be the place where the doctor revealed that he was indeed a wizard and then shared with him all the secrets of how to defeat Monsters. Or gave him a powerful sword or Ward of Protection or something.

But being told he wasn't crazy—and knowing that the doctor would tell his mom he wasn't crazy—was also a nice turn of events.

"If you don't mind me asking, Clark...I'm just curious. If the stuffed animals are to keep away the monsters at night... why do you carry a stuffed animal with you during the day?"

Clark thought carefully.

There was a broom closet on the way to the boys' bathroom at school. When you had to go during class and the halls were completely empty and silent...well, it looked like the door could just swing open, revealing shadowy horrors behind it.

There was a weird cluster of sickly-looking bushes in a corner of the school yard surrounded by a ring of dust and dead-packed dirt that all the kids just sort of stayed away from. *All* the kids. Even seventh graders.

There was the walk from the bus to his house and the ramshackle little cage the Bradburies kept their garbage cans in. It was always locked and had chicken wire on the front like a prison. Clark had once hurried past it and then looked behind him—and saw that the gate on it was suddenly ajar. There was no one around.

"He makes me feel better. Safe. Even if I'm not safe—from bullies." Clark added the last bit quickly.

The doctor raised an eyebrow. He might not actually have been a wizard after all, but he could read minds and detect lies like one.

Clark flew out of the room happier than he probably should have been. But he knew other kids who saw Talk Doctors and was pretty sure that *their* doctors didn't tell them there was nothing wrong with them.

He tried to listen in on his mother's conversation with the doctor/wizard behind the office door but couldn't hear anything. All he picked up were tense, short words from his mom and soothing but firm tones from the doctor.

Clark's mother stalked out and he trailed behind. He had a feeling he would never see the doctor again, which was almost a shame—in the end, he had seemed sort of nice.

EIGHT

Still Day

When they arrived at Ithaqua Gelato, Anna and Grandma were already there, chatting like two old girlfriends over sundaes. Clark practically leaped out of the car and into his grandmother's arms with the force of a tiny linebacker.

"Heya, Clark," she said, smiling and panting only a little. Grandma Machen wore jeans and T-shirts but also what she called crazy-little-old-lady hats. The one she had on today was white straw with roses. She had short hair and twinkling black eyes and was most likely the best grandma on the planet.

"I gave your sister some old perfume I never use," she said.

Anna held up a tiny glass cylinder of something labeled *Noir* and whispered triumphantly, *"This is the bomb."*

"Let's see what I have for you..." Grandma continued, whistling through her teeth. "Oh, look."

Out of her giant purse—which already seemed to hold more

things than it possibly should—she pulled a beanbag dog. He was white and gray and had little sharp white teeth embroidered on the sides of his mouth. Somehow it was both cute and ferocious-looking.

Two for being medium-size, Clark thought. *Plus one for the fangs . . .*

"Oh for heaven's sake, Mother," Mrs. Smith said. "I thought I told you—"

"Thanks, Grandma! Is it a wolf puppy?"

"It is indeed. I got it from a nature charity I give money to. I think his name is White Fang. But I don't think he's an arctic wolf. And you can call him whatever you like, of course."

Clark took the floppy Stuffy and wondered if there was a plus one somewhere for being a wolf—a naturally fierce creature. Unlike a horse or bunny.

"How's Bob, dear?" Grandma asked his mom as he and White Fang began looking over the ice-cream choices.

"He's . . . fine," Mrs. Smith answered, also studying the menu.

"'Fine?'" Grandma asked sharply.

"Oh, I don't know. He's a little burned-out, I think. In a rut. Tired. Something. He doesn't have any *ooomph.*"

"You know, it might finally all be catching up with him," Grandma Machen suggested. "You told me that he never saw anyone for what went on in his childhood. Maybe getting a box of memorabilia from his past brought up old memories. Ghosts. Bad vibes."

"Don't be silly! It's just a slump," Mrs. Smith said with a smile—but her lips pressed firmly together at the end. "What about you? How's your..." She motioned at her chest, alluding to the operation her mother'd had a month ago. That was Clark's first trip to the hospital except for the time he couldn't stop throwing up.

"Oh, it's healing all right. I start the rest of the stuff soon. But we can talk about that on the phone later." Grandma Machen sighed, waving her hand. "Let's not ruin the day."

"Okay. I'm going to run to the restroom. Clark, wash your hands when I come out."

He waited until his mom was fully in the bathroom and the old-fashioned lock clicked closed before he turned to his grandma.

"What about Dad's childhood? What happened?" If Monsters could only really hurt children, maybe something had happened back then that was somehow still hurting him now.

"It's really not for me to talk about."

But she didn't deny there *was* something. Anna was also listening with interest. "Let's just say your father didn't have it easy growing up. And sometimes that can leave scars."

Scars? Or Monsters? What if his dad didn't have enough action figures or stuffed animals or toy soldiers or whatever to protect him? And what *about* that box he got from Grandma and Grandpa Smith? What if a Monster had somehow managed to survive all these years... and snuck into the package of old things, along with everything else?

"Is that why you give me so many stuffed animals?" he whispered. "To keep me safe?"

Grandma Machen leaned over and tweaked him on the nose, rolling her eyes.

But she didn't deny it.

Most of the way home Mrs. Smith was silent. Finally, as they turned onto Carcosa Avenue, she cleared her throat. "I think, if you guys behave, your dad will take tomorrow off and we'll all go to the reservoir."

Clark and Anna both shouted: "WAHOO!"

"This is great," Anna whispered to Clark. "Whatever you're doing, keep it up!"

But that evening, while Clark introduced White Fang to everyone in bed and worked on different potential arrangements of his Stuffies, he heard his parents shouting. Actually, just his mom. His dad's voice was nearly silent and unintelligible.

"Come on, just..."

"nfgnnfngf."

"I promised the kids..."

"ngfgfmmmg."

"Don't you dare pull a no-show...."

In her room, Anna turned up her music.

Clark said his good nights and felt exhaustion descend....

And then suddenly his eyes shot open. He sat up, a strange and wonderful idea sprouting in his head.

"Sorry, Draco," he whispered to his dragon. "I think you're needed elsewhere tonight."

Before he could change his mind, Clark hopped out of bed

with the large Stuffy and tiptoed down the superdark hall. Anna's creepy dolls sat on her pillows, their black eyes glittering in what little light there was. Clark didn't like them, but at least they were guarding her.

When he reached his parents' door he—ever-so-quietly—reached out and gently placed Draco on the floor in front of it, facing out.

"Guard them well," Clark ordered.

Then he ran back to his room as fast as tippy-toes would allow. He leaped into bed and pulled the sheets over his head, gave Snowy and White Fang—the two newbies—a comforting pat, then curled up and pulled Winkum to him.

This time he was asleep almost immediately, a secret smile on his lips.

NINE

Day

"Come on, everybody! Out to the car—Clark, darn it, how many times have I told you to not to leave your stuffed animals lying around?"

Clark's mom scooped up Draco, who had been doing nothing at all besides sitting politely in front of the door of her bedroom. Clark managed to hide a smug little smile as he took the dragon and gave him a squeeze and a once-over.

Nothing looked scratched, torn, or out of place. Maybe the dragon just looked so fierce that it was enough to scare any Monsters off.

"Good job, buddy," he whispered. "Do it again tonight, huh?"

Having Draco there *must* have kept the enemy at bay; there was no protest at all from Mr. Smith this morning as his wife click-clacked around in her shiny red sandals and swooshed in her bright blue beach cover-up. He himself moved slowly and was dreadfully pale, but actually responded when people said things and did his bit to pack up the car.

He didn't drive; he didn't seem up for it. But that was okay. Clark loved all of them being together in the family car. He loved that his mom wasn't wearing her phone earpiece like she always did (although he caught her holding it in her fingers, playing with it and spinning it like she couldn't let it go).

He loved that Anna was in the backseat with him like they were both proper kids.

She was, of course, all in black: her new bathing suit, a new black hat with an exceedingly wide brim, her curlicue sunglasses, black fake-wood Japanese clogs. Clark had on a pair of blue board shorts and a comfy Baja, and two bright white stripes of sunblock on his cheeks—but he didn't care. They felt like a real family, like on TV or in the movies.

It was a cloudless, perfect summer day. The giant pine trees that marked the edge of the reservoir stretched high into infinity. A few families had already begun to set up on picnic tables beneath them, but most people preferred the sunny beach area. The Smiths picked their usual spot on the far edge of the swim zone; it was quieter there, and a very interesting stream burbled nearby. They laid out the blue-checked blanket for the kids and the red-checked one for Mr. and Mrs. Smith and the picnic lunch supplies. And then they turned their attention to having fun.

Anna barely dipped her toes in the water, preferring to pose on the pine-needle-strewn lawn with her parasol. Mrs. Smith did get her to play a few rounds of badminton—but she insisted on using her folded-up parasol, not a proper racket. Clark went in the chilly water immediately, all the way to his chest for as long as he could stand it. Around the edges of the lake were fish and sometimes turtles and frogs and good muddy things to poke a stick at. Sometimes there were newts that hung perfectly in the water, halfway between the surface and the bottom. They looked like tiny dragons.

Mrs. Smith pulled out a stack of magazines she never allowed herself to read during workdays. Mr. Smith also stayed on the blanket, just sitting and watching the kids. His legs were drawn up almost to his chest, but he looked content.

"Hey, Dad," Anna called out. "Why don't you show us how a *real man* goes swimming in a freezing cold lake."

Clark wondered if he was the only one who could hear the nervousness in her voice. How afraid she was of him saying no.

But Mr. Smith gave a wan smile and stood up, taking off his shirt.

Clark gasped.

His dad's back, up near his neck, was covered with dozens of red marks. *Pairs* of little red marks—tiny scabs that were healing over.

None of the wounds were fresh. None of them were from the night before, when Draco was guarding the door.

"Holy crow, Bob," his wife said, shocked.

"What?" he said, not even doing that thing where you try

to look around at the back of your own neck and can't. "It's just mosquito bites. Or something."

"Those aren't mosquito bites, Dad," Anna said, coming closer. "Those are *puncture wounds.*"

"Don't be so dramatic, Anna," their mom snapped. But she didn't look less worried. "God, I hope it's not bedbugs. It cannot be bedbugs. The Hope-Hodgsons had bedbugs. They had to throw *everything* out."

"Whatever. I'm going in," Mr. Smith declared. Then he took off, cannonballing into the murky depths the way he used to.

Mrs. Smith burst out laughing.

"Bob!" she called. "You could have hurt your head!"

Soon they were all in the lake, splashing each other. Even Anna. Somehow she managed to keep her sunglasses on the whole time. Mrs. Smith practiced the breaststroke and pretended to drown her husband. Mr. Smith picked up Clark and threw him, laughing, into the cold black water.

But later, as he tried to dry out and the sun didn't seem to do any good, Clark worried about the night. He had to ask D. A. about the wounds and what kind of Monster was feeding on his dad. The other boy would certainly know what was going on and how to stop it. Permanently.

"Mom? When can I have a playdate with D. A. again?" he asked.

"Not soon," his mother answered distractedly, tightening a

lid onto a plastic container of macaroni salad. "He's...at camp right now. Sleepaway camp."

"Oh." Clark was terribly disappointed. His new friend hadn't said anything about going to camp. When would he be back?

"In fact..." his mother continued slowly, as if she was just deciding something, "you're going to that camp, too."

Clark gave her a look. Camp was always a complete failure— and that was just day camp. *Sleepaway* camp? Nope. Forget it.

On the other hand, if D. A. were there...

"It's called Camp I Can," his mother continued. She spoke faster now, and firmly, like she had just made up her mind and was happy with it. "You'll make all sorts of new friends, go on hikes, canoe on a big lake, do crafts...all while learning self-reliance and improving your social skills. After just one week at Camp I Can, you will leave more confident and more adventurous!"

Clark was fairly certain, from her tone of voice, that she was quoting a brochure she had memorized.

Seven perfect days of summer in a row.

Ruined.

TEN

Night

Clark was woken up by...*something*. Some noise. Some fading memory of a noise. It sounded like paper rustling against something metal. It sounded like feathers soaked in oil and dragged along the floor. It sounded like nothing he could—or wanted to—describe.

He quickly counted all of his Stuffies. *Thirteen*. Why was there an extra one?

Draco.

He was thrown on top of those guarding his left side. When he should have been in the doorway of his parents' room, guarding *them*.

His mom must have found him and put him "back."

Clark leaned up on one elbow and looked out over the room.

His carefully arranged flanks of Stuffies were scattered, strewn across the floor like a wind had swept through.

It *could* have been his mom. When she came back to return Draco.

Slrrrpp

Clark turned his head in time to see a long shadow slip through the crack of his door, out into the hall.

It *could* have been the shadow of someone's legs on the way to the bathroom, made longer by the light at the other end of the hall.

Clark strained to listen. The house was dead silent. No clocks ticked. Anna wasn't even snoring like she usually did.

But both kids were safe, protected by their dolls and Stuffies.

While he was at camp Clark would be separated from his dad for over a week. With no way to protect him.

For the first time ever, Clark wasn't just terrified for himself.

For the first time he was terrified for his parents.

FOON

poor Clark and Clark's dad. i was but
I wasnt <u>there</u> yet. i was beginning
to being. if i was completely was
and there i cud of helped.

ELEVEN

Days

The next morning Mr. Smith didn't even get out of bed.

Clark quietly cursed to himself using one of his mom's Forbidden Words. He had to get better at hiding Stuffies in front of his parents' room.

No, wait, maybe *in* his parents' room!

His mom wouldn't be able to find them all, if there were enough. One in his dad's drawer. One under the bed. One outside the window...

Of course doing so would mean reducing his own ranks, which was worrisome.

And they were all too big and easily found.

And he could only do it until he left for camp. Then he would have to figure out something else.

Unless...

What was it D. A. had said? *Handmade Stuffies are the most* powerful. And *When you give them to people they sort of have to put it on their bags or purses or phones or whatever.*

Eureka!

"What are you doing?" Mrs. Smith asked.

Clark had several pieces of scrap felt in one hand, white cotton batting from a vitamin jar in the other, and a very guilty look on his face.

He was standing in front of the corkboard where his mom stuck inspirational quotes, coupons, tickets, pictures of the kids, and loose pins and needles. Some of the needles already had thread sticking out their ends, ready to go if there was a mending emergency the morning before school or work.

"I just want to make something for Dad," Clark said as pitifully as he could. "To remind him of me when I'm at camp. To take wherever he goes. You know, he just seems...so... down...."

All true.

Also if he said those sorts of things, his dad would be touched and do whatever he asked, like keeping a tiny Clark-made Stuffy with him at all times. For instance.

Like that time his mom wore that realllllly ugly rose pin he made for her out of Sculpey. He was five and begged her to show it off to all her friends. Mrs. Smith proudly kept it on the collar of her shirts for a month despite the fact that it looked exactly like a wad of spit-out bubblegum.

"Oh," she said, lips quivering. "That's so sweet!"

She hugged Clark to her, which was a little much. Her arms

were strong, her kiss on his cheek solid. He had no trouble imagining her pulling out a sword and dispatching any demonic evildoers who might try to attack her kids. Fierce and effective, just the way D. A. described Snowy. Just like Grandma Machen, in her own quiet little way.

So why wasn't his mom enough to keep Monsters away from his dad?

A week passed. Camp came despite the silent prayers Clark added to his whispered list of good nights.

And even worse, his camp uniform was mind-blowingly stupid.

Beige shorts that were way too long and a bright purple shirt with CAMP I CAN in childish yellow bubble letters.

"It's not purple. It's *Vehement Violet!*" his mom insisted.

"It's pretty much completely purple, Mom," Anna said. "I mean, *I* would call it amaranthine, but I doubt anyone else would."

The rest of his stupid uniforms would be waiting for him at camp, along with Camp I Can Real Camper-Made Soap and Shampoo. Also packed in his approved white duffel daypack (with no dangles or logos) was a towel, flip-flops for the showers, sheets, a pillowcase, two (2) bathing suits of appropriate size and coverage, underwear, socks, and a plain pair of sneakers.

For personal belongings the camp allowed books (no unapproved series, no movie or TV licenses), a journal and a pencil, religious jewelry (none for Clark, though Anna had tried to make him wear a giant black pentagram), a brush, and razors (for the older campers). No Stuffies, no plastic figurines, no makeup, no music, no deodorant (for the older campers). And no electronics!

"It's like he's joining the army," Anna said, looking at Clark's pitifully small bags.

"No, they do this on purpose, to"—Mrs. Smith held up the brochure and read it aloud—"'foster equality between the campers and erase distinctions between class and background. *Everyone* is friends at Camp I Can!'"

Anna scanned the text over her mom's shoulder. "It doesn't say anything there about stuffed animals. They mean just, like, fancy jeans and gang colors."

Mrs. Smith shrugged and smiled brightly. "Oh, well, I read it somewhere. Not in this brochure. A different one."

Then she narrowed her eyes at Clark. He realized a second too late that he wasn't protesting enough.

At all, really.

He tried to look innocent.

"Give me the bag, Clark," she ordered.

Clark sighed and held it out.

Anna shot him a sympathetic look.

His mom quickly and efficiently emptied its contents out on the table. Kevin and Winkum rolled out immediately. White Fang was tucked between pairs of underwear.

He wilted while she put everything but the stuffed animals back in his bag.

"You are going to learn to be independent. To grow up and put away childish habits."

At the end of each sentence she shoved something into his bag particularly hard for emphasis.

Clark watched her, fuming. He had never spent a night away from home and family before—except at Grandma Machen's. And here they were sending him off for a whole week to someplace he had never been. Scary wood cabins? In a bunk by himself at night? *Him?*

"*I DON'T WANT TO GO TO CAMP!*" he finally exploded. "*YOU'RE MAKING ME GO AND NOT EVEN LETTING ME TAKE A FRIEND!*"

"They are *not* friends. They are just toys, Clark," his mom said. "You will make real friends at camp. Human ones. I'm doing this because I love you, Clark. You need this."

"If you really loved me, you wouldn't ship me off to stay with strangers for a week," Clark growled. Actually growled. He had never talked to his parents that way before.

His mother's eyes widened with hurt. Like she had never considered how he might actually, really feel.

For just a moment Clark didn't care. She needed to know how upset he was.

Anna flicked open her black lace fan and began fanning herself nervously, watching the two of them with big manga eyes.

The standoff was broken by a cheery voice calling from the front step.

"Claaaaark!"

Grandma Machen swept in with a fresh breeze, her yellow T-shirt brightening the room like sunshine. Today her crazy-little-old-lady hat was a baseball cap with a pink ribbon on it for the cancer she had.

"How's my little super grown-up camper?"

She bent down and squeezed his cheeks—she always said she did it as a joke, "ironically." So Clark didn't mind. But she did kiss him, leaving bright spots of nice-smelling lip gloss on his skin.

"Oh my goodness, I remember the first time we sent your mother to camp. She *howled....*"

"Mother," Mrs. Smith hissed.

"Oh, she loved it in the end," Grandma Machen finished sweetly. "You will, too. Change is hard. Believe me. I'm afraid while you're at camp I start my chemo for this nasty cancer. So we'll both be miserable."

"MOTHER!" Mrs. Smith exploded.

But her mother ignored her. She pulled out a tiny shopping bag and handed it to Clark. "We'll both come out of it fine. Besides, look what I made you for the occasion!"

Clark reached into the bag curiously....

And pulled out what might have been the ugliest stuffed animal he had ever seen.

It looked like it was cobbled together from socks. But not

like a sock monkey. Or maybe like several sock monkeys gone horribly wrong. Melded together in some tragic sock-monkey disaster.

It had two short fat hind legs and a neck that was too long and narrow. It had a wide face full of teeth and what looked like a giant pair of tusks. It had a pair of not-quite-matching horns on its head. Or maybe they were bunny ears. It had buttons from a leather coat for eyes and a tiny pair of useless-looking arms that clutched a little spear-shaped plastic drink-stirrer. He was just about every dull color and pattern dull adult socks were made from.

"Geez Louise," Mrs. Smith said in disgust. "What the heck is that thing, Mom?"

"His name is Foon," Grandma Machen said with great dignity.

"Foon?"

"Remember your old fluffy rabbit, the fat one, that was almost perfectly round and puffed up like a balloon? *Fluffy balloon?* You called her Foon, because that was too hard for you to say."

Clark gave his mom a look. *She* had a Stuffy? And she named it *Foon?*

Mrs. Smith looked straight ahead, her face struggling between guilty and embarrassed.

"Anyway, this is Foon, too," Grandma Machen said with a pleasant smile. Maybe more *smug* than pleasant. "I'm not the best at arts-and-craftsy things, Clark. You know that. Except for whittling. But I can promise you he was made with a lot of love."

Clark turned Foon over in his hands. Sure, he was ugly. But he was sturdily stitched. And he had fangs . . . and horns . . . and his little weapon. Adding up the points, Foon was at least a *nine.* Higher than any of his other stuffed animals.

It was almost like his grandmother *knew* somehow. . . .

"I thought you could take him to camp with you. As a mascot," she said with an innocent look on her face.

"Mother," Mrs. Smith said tightly, "I believe I told you. Explicitly. No toys or stuffed animals.*"*

"Who said anything about a toy or a stuffed animal?" Grandma Machen said, continuing to look innocent. But there was a hard edge to her voice. "I said he's a mascot. And I'm sure whatever silly rules the camp has can be set aside considering the circumstances. A stuffed mascot, handmade by a loving grandma, who . . . well, who has certain *circumstances* in her own life . . . *cancer,* you know . . ."

Mrs. Smith wilted.

Clark was torn between throwing his arms around his grandma and keeping still and shutting up and waiting to see if he could take the Stuffy with him. As ugly as Foon was, at that moment he was the most beautiful thing in the world.

Clark shot a guilty look at his other Stuffies. He hoped they understood.

"Ehh," Mrs. Smith finally said, a strange nonword for her. She almost never had trouble saying one thing or the other. This made-up, in-between thing was highly unusual.

Grandma Machen smiled wider, and even more sweetly, if

that was possible. She tapped the little pink ribbon on her hat, as if fixing it.

Clark's mom finally gave up. "Whatever. I guess it's okay."

"Of course it is," Grandma Machen said, giving Clark a little wink. "You take care of him, now!"

But she was saying it to Foon, not her grandchild.

In the backseat of the car, Clark looked out the window and tried to decide how to feel. It was definitely an adventure, like the ones his stuffed animals always had. And this was way less dangerous than the ones he usually imagined. All he was really doing was going off to a new place and camping with a bunch of people he didn't know. Not attacking castles or escaping Star Destroyers. If only the sun didn't keep glaring off the shiny yellow letters on his purple shirt. No one wore dumb shirts on great quests.

Anna spent the ride with her nose in her phone.

"Hey." Clark poked her.

"What's up, squirt?" she asked without looking up.

"Can you do me a favor? It's a weird one."

"You have my attention," she said, immediately putting her phone in the tiny velvet satchel that dangled from her elbow.

"Can you . . . can you hide three stuffed animals in Mom and Dad's room every night? Like, at least one, but three would be better. White Fang, Snowy if she fits somewhere, and Kevin?"

Anna blinked at him. Whatever weird thing she was expecting, this surpassed it.

"It's kind of like a spell," Clark said, fishing for words that Anna would understand. "To keep Mom and Dad safe while I'm gone."

"To keep Mom and Dad safe. Stuffed animals. I get it." Anna nodded as if it made sense. Then she quickly covered this reaction with a sneer. "What about me? *I* don't rate a stuffed animal?"

"You *have* Stuffies. And your awful dolls," Clark pointed out. He made a point to look at the giant black bag between them, that was pretty much over the line on his side—and its giant chain of charms and things. At home, besides her ball-jointed vampire-girl dolls, she also always slept with a giant fanged bunny named Siouxsie and a pillow rock star called Fat Bob.

"Point taken," she agreed. "All right, weirdo, if that's what you want, I'll do it. Secret mission. Covert ops. I'm all in."

Clark had one horrifying vision of his sister wearing leggings, all-black like a ninja, a mask over her face, trying to disappear into a shadow that was much too small for her. After spending hours picking out just the right matte black nail polish.

But still, it was a relief. She would have his back. He could trust her.

TWELVE

Day

As the little car drove up the side of a wide green hill, Camp I Can appeared: cabins and parking lots and a mossy line of pine trees rolling closer like a bright inevitability.

Clark leaned forward despite himself, trying to take it all in. The camp didn't look at all terrifying or ominous or like something out of a horror movie.

A smiling young man in a *yellow* T-shirt with *purple* letters who was holding a clipboard approached their car and directed them where to park. A smiling young woman also in a yellow T-shirt and holding a clipboard directed Clark where to put his linens bag: on a tarp labeled ICANCABIN12: SUNFISH. Another smiling young woman in a yellow T-shirt with a clipboard led them into the camp itself.

"It's totally a cult," Anna murmured from behind her large

sunglasses. Both her parasol and her fan were out, protecting her from the sun.

"Stuff it, Miss Smith!" Mrs. Smith snapped. She was looking around interestedly, her head craning back and forth like a happy puppy. Mr. Smith also looked around, albeit with a bit more confusion. Sometimes he scratched under his collar at the bite marks there.

And sometimes he played with the little Stuffy on his keychain, the one Clark made that mostly looked like a bear.

The Smiths joined other families with interested parents and reluctant campers in a slow marching tour of the camp, unable to hear a thing the chirpy, smiling young woman in the yellow shirt said.

They passed a canteen, a cafeteria, a picturesque beach on an enormous lake with an old-looking boat dock. They passed campers staying there for the whole summer, many of whom were engaged in a game that seemed to mainly involve throwing burdock burrs into each other's hair. They passed the main office, which had a giant chalkboard outside with fun announcements colored in rainbow pastel chalks. None of it exuded an undercurrent of terror. The burdock-burr game looked kind of fun. It was strange how even older campers were involved, like it wasn't a silly game beneath their notice.

The tour ended at a natural amphitheater in the bowl of two small hills, soft and filled with rust-colored pine needles. The families sat on benches beneath the giant trees, and Clark took a deep breath. It smelled like peace.

Monsters didn't stand a chance in a place like this.

"WELCOME TO CAMP I CAN AND LAKE WANTA-STIQUET!" a smiling older man shouted through a megaphone. The only people who clapped were parents and counselors.

"NOW I KNOW PARTING CAN BE A DIFFICULT TIME, SO LET'S MAKE IT SHORT AND SWEET, FAMILIES! A GREAT WEEK IS BEGINNING FOR YOUR CAMPERS AND WE DON'T WANT THEM TO MISS A SECOND!"

Clark's stomach spasmed in panic. This was it. His parents were really going to leave him. Here. Under these pines, by this—okay, gorgeous—lake, with these weird people in yellow shirts. The trees were nice, but he was going to be *alone*. Nothing would change about this situation; nothing he could say or do would make a difference at this point.

He felt the sudden little pain behind his eyes that meant tears were going to come. The only thing that could possibly make things worse.

And then the older man was done speaking and Clark turned to formally say good-bye to his parents—and saw that his mom's eyes were also bright. Shiny bright and wet. She lifted her hand to fiddle with her ear, but her earpiece wasn't there, of course.

She was *also* upset by saying good-bye. She didn't want to send him off!

She just actually, really for reals thought this was for his own good. She was sending him away even though it hurt her, too.

That didn't exactly make things better for Clark, but it did stop him from crying.

"Bye," he whispered, not trusting his voice. He hugged his mom tight, then his dad.

"Bye, squirt," his sister said, ruffling his hair. "Don't eat the meat. I'll bet it's like grade-D."

"Anna," her mother said in a warning tone.

"First sleepover camp," Mr. Smith said, sounding slightly surprised. As if the entire family hadn't been gearing up for it for days. "Have a great week, buddy. See you on the other side."

The other side of *what*? Clark wanted to ask, but Mr. Smith put his arms around his girls' shoulders and they walked away, looking from the back like a three-headed Monster.

Clark wanted to run after them, but they were soon lost in the dusty crowds of campers and families and counselors.

"HI, BUDDY, DO YOU KNOW WHERE YOU'RE GOING?" a smiling medium-aged man in a yellow shirt asked. Clark decided he preferred the teenage counselors. Their smiles seemed more honest.

"Sunfish Cabin?" he said hesitantly.

"OH, WOW, ALREADY AN OLD HAND AT THIS! HIGH-FIVE!"

Clark didn't have the nerve to leave the man hanging; he seemed so desperate. Reluctantly he reached up and tapped the man's palm. Then he used the moment when the man went to look back down at his clipboard to tiptoe away.

The grounds were chaos: Families were picking up kids from the previous session, laundry and food and mail were being delivered in slow-rolling vans, new campers, shell-shocked—and sometimes crying—wandered around looking lost despite the helpful people in the yellow shirts.

Wait, was that...?

"D. A.!"

His new friend was there, too! He was with his mom and dad, as sturdy and solid as ever, in a dusty camp shirt and with a pack over his back. He wore, despite camp regulations, his usual baseball cap.

The other boy's face broke out into an enormous grin when he saw who called him. Clark felt like a million dollars.

"Clark! Holy crow! I can't believe we missed each other like this. This *stinks!*" he swore cheerfully.

"D. A.," his mother said sternly. "Hello, Clark."

"Missed?" Clark asked.

"Yeah, I only had one session here and it's over. Geez, I wish our parents coulda coordinated better."

"We have to go," D. A.'s father said. "We have to bring D. A. to baseball camp now and registration closes at four."

"Sorry," D. A.'s mother said. "Another playdate, another time?" Without waiting for an answer she took her son firmly by the hand and started to walk away.

"Go see Catherine-Lucille!" D. A. called over his shoulder. "In the Crafts Cabin. Make sure you talk to her. *Catherine-Lucille.* She knows everything!"

Clark watched his friend disappear into the crowd and felt the opposite of whatever it was he felt before. For about five seconds he potentially had this wonderful thing—a friend at camp—and then watched as that wonderful thing exploded into a million drippy pieces.

Still, D. A. had tried to help him out. *Catherine-Lucille.* He would find her.

"HEY, BUDDY. YOU SEEM LOST. WHY AREN'T YOU AT YOUR CABIN MAKING FRIENDS?"

Clark couldn't be entirely certain, but he was *fairly* certain the person speaking to him now was the same one who had spoken to him before. But there was no recognition in the man's eyes. Clark decided not to argue and let the person or robot guide him to Sunfish Cabin without protest.

"OKAY, LOOKS LIKE YOU'RE SIGNED UP FOR A SWIM TEST TOMORROW AND THEN CANOE-ING AND THEN ORIENTEERING AND THEN FIRE SKILLS AND GROUP RAP IN THE AFTERNOON," the counselor said, checking his clipboard.

"What about Crafts?" Clark asked.

"YOU'RE NOT SIGNED UP FOR THAT."

"Oh."

They were both silent for a moment. The man continued to smile.

"Well..." Clark ventured, "*could* I be? Signed up?"

The counselor continued to stare at him blankly for another long moment.

"OF COURSE!" he finally said with a great grin, like it was the best idea in the world. "AMAZING INITIATIVE, BUDDY! ASKING FOR THINGS! YOU'RE SURE, THOUGH? YOU'D HAVE TO GIVE UP FIRE SKILLS."

That was too bad. Fire Skills *did* sound cool. But finding Catherine-Lucille was more important.

"I'm sure. I like crafts."

"OKAY, YOUR WORD IS MY COMMAND! CRAFTS IT IS!" He scribbled something down on his clipboard. "AND HERE WE ARE! WELCOME TO YOUR NEW HOME!"

He presented the cabin with an arm wave like he was revealing a glorious castle.

Sunfish Cabin was small, wood, brown, and dark. The word *Sunfish* was sloppily hand lettered above the door. It had screens instead of proper windows, and the screens had holes in them. Mosquito-size holes.

Clark pushed the creaky screen door inward. There were eight bunks and no electric lights inside. It smelled. It was even hotter than outside. Everyone's belongings had been arranged on beds already: Clark got a lower bunk.

Several campers were sitting on their unmade beds, hands twitching a little, staring at one another. At first Clark thought that a couple of them were playing a game like Pokémon or even rock paper scissors, but there was nothing actually *in* their hands. On closer inspection it looked like they were hitting buttons on imaginary video game controllers while trying to maintain normal conversations.

It was a mixed group; a couple of girls had come over from their cabins.

"What are you in for?" one boy immediately asked Clark. His eyes looked hollow.

"Um? A week?"

"No, like what's your . . . *'exciting challenge to overcome'*?" another boy asked, saying the last part sarcastically. He had a backward baseball cap on. "Mine's TV. I watch, like, five, six hours a day."

"I'm in for p-ponies," one girl said. She had tiny black pigtails and was shaking a little more than the others. "They said I had too many ponies. I just . . . I just *like* ponies."

"Video games," the other girl said. "They cut me off cold turkey. So what's your deal?"

If he admitted it was stuffed animals, would they make fun of him? Wedgie him? Beat him up?

"Too many, uh, action figures. Mostly Star Wars." It wasn't a complete lie. While his parents approved of the action figures more than the stuffed animals, they still thought he had too many of the hard-plastic animal variety (not stormtroopers, of course) and complained when he left them out on the floor for them to step on.

"Ohhhh yeah," a third boy said. "It's . . . uh . . . *action figures* for me, too."

"What about you?" Clark asked the first boy.

"Petty theft. I boosted ten packs of Pokémon cards from the drug store." He said it with a shrug.

Wow, a real live criminal. Sitting right there. Before Clark could think about this for too long, the girl with the pigtails suddenly grabbed his arm.

"CAN YOU DRAW?"

"A little? I guess?" He tried to pull away from her cold fingers.

"CAN YOU DRAW A PONY?"

She gazed at him with big beseeching brown eyes. Everyone else in the room looked away in embarrassment.

"I guess?"

The poor girl seemed so desperate. He couldn't say no.

She handed him a pad of paper with some pretty execrable attempts on it: One halfway-decent horse still looked like a sick cross between a balloon and a stick figure. Clark wasn't a great artist, but he could do spaceships and dragons okay. He thought about Dark Horse and Winkum, and the ponies on the TV show. Then he very carefully drew a puffy little horse with short legs, a nice mane and tail. The eyes were huge and terrible, but he was never good at making eyes look smart. As a final touch he drew a cheery sun on the pony's visible flank.

The girl took the picture from him with great delicacy: a hastily drawn sketch of questionable skill on a torn piece of paper. Her eyes were wide with awe.

"Thank you," she whispered. She brushed the pony's mane with her fingertips. "I just... I just needed a pony."

Then she got up and stumbled back to her own cabin, never taking her eyes off the picture.

☆ ☆ ☆

After a truly stupid name-learning game led by a bored leader-in-training, it was time for dinner. TACO NIGHT! cheerful placards announced.

Counselors chanted:

"TACO NIGHT, TACO NIGHT! GONNA BE A SALSA FIGHT! EAT YER BEANS AND EAT YER CHIPS, BUT DONCHOO EVER DOUBLE DIPS!"

"I'll bet it's only good the first night," Backward-Baseball-Cap Boy muttered. "To keep us hopeful." He wasn't actually from Sunfish Cabin, so Clark hadn't learned his name.

Clark eyed the vat of reddish ground "meat filling" and skipped it, thinking about what Anna had said.

After a group recitation of something that sounded a whole lot like grace but didn't mention God, everyone dug in, arguing and laughing and talking loudly and bravely. For dessert there was chocolate pudding and a lot of poop jokes.

Afterward there were more group songs and a recitation of how the next day would go and a reminder to put on clean underwear in the morning. Also there was mention of a stuffed platypus hidden somewhere in one of the main public cabins and whoever found it would win a bag of candy from the canteen.

All of this, all the songs and games and whatever else, were to keep the campers busy and unable to think about how far they were from home. It was completely obvious. The counselors did a pretty good job, Clark admitted—but they weren't perfect.

He felt a pang and wished he had one of those terrible nutritious granola cookies his mom made, the ones with a thumbprint of jam on the top instead of chocolate.

When they went to their separate cabins the sun was a golden smudge behind a line of black pine trees. Pony Girl— Clark never caught her name—found him and threw her arms around his neck. She still had the drawing he had made earlier carefully held in her left fist.

"Thanks again," she whispered. Her eyes were dark and haunted.

"Why didn't you just *sneak* a pony in? Like in your shirt, or something?" Clark asked, uncomfortable but unable to contain his curiosity. Ponies were pretty small, after all.

"I did!" she wailed. "My mom found it and took it before she left!"

A surprisingly familiar story. Clark wondered how many other campers had the exact same experience.

The girl ran off into the dark, sniffling.

A couple boys from Sunfish saw this interaction. Clark blushed but concentrated on ponies to distract himself. The ones you could buy were pretty small, as small as beanbags, but they were plastic. Did that make them a two or three? Some of them had unicorn horns which was another plus one. If some had *sustainably imagined* magic that was easily another plus one. And if that girl had a small army of them... Well, she and her family were quite safe.

The campers all brushed their teeth at the one water trough

between the cabins. Clark timed his trip to the outhouse so he was slightly behind some of the other kids. He wouldn't have to go back alone in the dark—but also wouldn't have to talk to anyone.

In bed they were allowed a few minutes of quiet time before lights out. Clark snuck Foon from his bag to under his covers, using the pretext of getting out his journal and pen. Writing a letter to his family was the closest thing he could think of to actually talking to them. They couldn't talk back, but it was better than nothing.

When he opened the journal a piece of folded paper fell out. It smelled faintly like laundry detergent.

Dear Clark,

Don't be homesick. We all love you and aren't that far away. Make friends and have fun!

Sweet Dreams,

Mom and Dad

Clark smiled but also felt like crying again. His heart beat warm and cold at the same time. He put the note under his pillow.

When he readied his pen to begin again, he saw faint words already on the page. Backward. Flipping four pages farther revealed a hastily scrawled note from his sister, the words biting deep into the paper from the sharp nib of the fountain pen she used.

MISSION INSTRUCTIONS RECEIVED. WILL FOLLOW ORDERS AS PLANNED.

GOOD LUCK, LIEUTENANT (pronounced LEFT-TENNANT, obviously).

Clark just felt warm this time, not sad, and decided to go to sleep with that feeling.

"Good night, Mom and Dad," he whispered. "And Anna and Grandma and Grandpa Smith and Grandma Machen and Grandpa Ken and Aaron and Nathan and Shantel yankeesrulesoxdrool and Superman and Batman and Wonder Woman."

He turned off his flashlight and snuggled down in his sleeping bag clutching Foon tight, hoping the warmth would carry him through to morning.

THIRTEEN

Night

Clark's eyes shot open in the blackness. He stayed as still as he could, frozen, terrified. Foon was still in the same place as when he fell asleep, nestled in his arm, almost under his armpit.

But where were all his other Stuffies? Where was Winkum, and the new guys—Snowy and White Fang? Where were Baz and Draco and Gribble and Kevin?

He panicked, feeling around the bed desperately.

Then he remembered.

Camp.

He wasn't alone in his bedroom. Boys all around him breathed loudly or snored lightly. The air smelled like pines. Real pines, not like the one that hung in their car from the rearview mirror. There was movement, but it wasn't of creepy shadows; it was someone turning over in his sleep.

There was absolutely nothing terrifying.

He was in a roomful of safe, warm—sometimes stinky—human bodies.

Clark gulped a sigh of relief and disappointment. It was a little confusing to wake in the middle of the night and not have any reason to be terrified. He was far from home, and that was terrible, and his parents weren't in the next room, and that was terrible, too, but there was nothing immediately or potentially dangerous nearby. There was no way a Monster could sneak around all of these kids.

And, Clark realized, at least one of the kids hugged something suspicious-looking—lumpy and soft—under the covers. Possibly a Stuffy. Possibly a pillow twisted and shaped into something that looked a whole lot like a Stuffy. That would be no good for defense.

Clark rolled over but thought about his parents.

They were far away from him...but he was far away from *them*. Would Anna keep her word? Would she protect them in his absence? Would his dad stay safe?

The scent of pines eventually lulled him into a fitful, troubled sleep.

FOON

this is where eye open
my ice for first time.

FOURTEEN

Day

Clark opened his eyes knowing exactly where he was this time.

Or rather, where he wasn't.

He knew he wasn't upstairs with his mom downstairs making some kooky, healthy breakfast. He knew he wasn't somewhere he could hear his sister snoring in the room next to him. He knew he wasn't somewhere he could easily check on the status of the Stuffy placement while his dad was in the nice bathroom with the good light, shaving for work.

These things may or may not have been happening at all. How could he tell, being so far away?

Clark swallowed exactly one wet, gasping breath that threatened to become something else. Then he got dressed facing his bed—most of the other boys did the same. He tucked Foon into his daypack and trotted off to the amphitheater along with, but not exactly *in*, the rest of the crowd. There was a flag-raising ceremony, which was weird. Everyone was very careful about unrolling the flag and not letting it touch the ground, and someone played a trumpet badly.

The moment the last trembling note sounded over the lake everyone made a mad dash for the mess tent. Apparently there was a limited number of sausages. The rest of breakfast was cold cereal, watery hot chocolate, and warm eggs that were both unnaturally fluffy and strangely granular at the same time.

Backward-Baseball-Cap Boy balanced five Cheerios on his nose.

Clark only managed three himself but cracked up with the other kids trying.

Afterward, Clark went to change for the swim test. His mom had packed his swim shirt. He hated wearing it.

But after sneaking a look around at the other boys, he realized something:

She wasn't there.

He didn't have to wear it.

Crazy!

He grabbed his towel and went down to the water. A short, dense fog still clung to the surface of the lake. The trees near the banks were squat and gnarled like drowning hands reaching up one last time for air. The water was blacker than death under the surface. Clark put a toe in. It was cold.

"OKAY, CAMP-I-CANNERS! EVERYONE INTO THE WATER!"

Some of the kids, fronting bravery, jumped straight off the dock. Clark forced his pale body into the dark, viscous water from the safety of the beach. The light from the sun looked strange in the fog. Everything was shades of gray.

The swim shirt probably would have prevented the goose bumps that crawled up his chest and back. But it was still stupid, and there were other freezing, shirtless boys in the water. Also freezing girls who didn't look any warmer for their tops.

It was all he could do to obey the megaphone words of the swim instructor. She did not herself get into the freezy cold lake. She wore a sweatshirt. Clark concentrated on paddling: one arm in front of the other, teeth chattering.

After two laps back and forth and two minutes treading water, he was awarded the rank of Eft. Which was better than Tadpole and worse than Leopard Frog.

His life jacket was borderline impossible to put on. He had to stand there like a much littler kid as the instructor yanked the straps and loudly showed him how to do it.

The girl who got to go in the front of the canoe was cute and had little Rebel Alliance beads in her cornrows and braids. But there wasn't any time to talk. Not between trying to hear the fog-muffled words of the instructor and trying to move the canoe forward a little—but mostly trying to avoid hitting one another in the head with the paddles.

In Orienteering, Clark got his own compass on a lanyard and had to find his way from one spot to the next. He came in twenty-fourth out of twenty-seven.

Chilly, still damp, depressed, and wishing he could just sit in a corner and cuddle Foon, Clark stumbled bravely on to Crafts. But before he could enter the bright mess of the cabin, Pokémon Thief found him.

"Hey, Clark! Where's your girlfriend?"

Clark sized up the boy; he was built like D. A. and Ben Eldritch, but larger, and stood with his hands at his hips, blocking the open door.

A real, live criminal. Not your average bully.

Clark tried to look around him to the inside of the cabin, but no one was paying attention. There didn't seem to be a counselor.

"What?" he asked, stalling.

"THE PONY GIRL. WHO WAS ALL HUGGGGGY AND TOUCCCCCHY WITH YOU LAST NIGHT. WE ALL SAW."

Pokémon Thief leaned forward in classic bully style, chin out. What would come next was inevitable: a verbal threat, then physical follow-up.

"SO. WHERE'S YOUR GIRLFRIEND?"

And then, something happened that was so extraordinary it changed Clark's view of the world forever.

Another voice called out sharply from the cabin. A *girl's* voice.

"*HIS* GIRLFRIEND? I GUESS YOU MEAN *YOUR MAMA*. AND *SHE'S* BACK AT YOUR HOUSE, MAKING UP TO YOUR DAD."

Pokémon Thief's eyes widened.

So did Clark's.

The girl appeared, hands also on hips, glaring at Pokémon Thief. Her thick brown hair hung in two long, old-fashioned pigtails down her back. The look in her dark eyes was pure evil.

"CATHERINE-LUCILLE!" came a warning adult voice from out of view.

"Sorry," the girl said promptly and contritely. "I truly apologize for suggesting that your mom was kissing this fellow camper of yours right here. That was wrong and utterly contrary to the focus of my exciting challenge to overcome. Now get lost before I do something to you that makes you *call* for your mama like the mewling sack of baby snot you are."

She said the last words perfectly clearly but very, *very* quietly, not altering her face or stance at all. A disinterested adult (or counselor) would have looked up and seen her doing something that seemed a lot like continuing to apologize.

Pokémon Thief turned red like a cartoon. Then he stomped off.

Clark let out the breath he had been holding. Before him sparkled a miracle. It was like the sun had come out and presented him with an angel in the form of a very angry little girl.

"Catherine-Lucille," he said. "D. A. told me to find you!"

"Yeah?" She looked him up and down with an interested eye, still not moving. "Yeah, you look like one of his finds. You look *haunted*, boy."

"I'm not…"

"You're haunted. Or someone in your family is."

She strode over to the worktable, beckoning him to follow. There were only other campers around it; the counselor was standing at the window, flirting with another counselor who was walking by with a box of confiscated home-baked cookies.

On the table were piles of felt, feathers and paint, and cloth, and a pincushion full of needles and a mason jar full of spools of thread. All the campers seated around it looked up at Catherine-Lucille attentively.

"At ease," she ordered. They immediately relaxed and went back to chatting among themselves and working on whatever little projects they had.

"You got any protection here?" she then asked, turning to Clark. "I know, I know," she said quickly, putting up her hand. "No Stuffies allowed, technically. But people sneak 'em in. Gotta ask."

"Um..."

He produced Foon out of his satchel and handed him to her.

"NICE," she said, turning the Stuffy over in her hands appreciatively. "Base three size, plus one each for the fangs and horns and claws and weapon, handmade is plus two.... Who made this for you?"

"My grandmother. She made it 'cause I was going to camp and..."

"Love. Plus two. Very nice. An eleven. Your granny sure knew what she was doing." She handed Foon back carefully, with respect.

Eleven? That was even higher than Clark had thought.

"I completely love the use of socks," she continued. "It's not my thing, but I appreciate good workmanship in any form."

"I'm hoping you can help me. I'm worried about my dad 'cause..."

"Sssshhh." Catherine-Lucille jerked her head at the counselor. "Not here, Private. Walls have ears. Let's get some work done and then meet after lunch for Quiet Time. Under the witch viburnum near the east path."

Clark looked at her blankly. He knew boxwood because he had asked his mom which plant smelled like cat pee. He knew pachysandra because he had asked his dad which plant it was that went on forever when he lost his action figures in it. He knew pansies.

He had no idea what witch viburnum was, but it sounded terrible.

Catherine-Lucille rolled her eyes.

"Bush with large heart-shaped leaves. You gotta get to know the native terrain if you want to survive, Private."

"Uh, heart-shaped leaves. Got it."

"All right, sit down and grab a needle. We got a *lot* of work to do here. None of these sorry cases here have anything. Guys or felties or zipper pulls or bag charms or Stuffies or *anything*. You got any skills?"

"Um, I made my dad a charm mascot thing...."

"*EXCELLENT*," she said, slapping him hard on the back. "You're a great asset to the team already."

And though the force of her blow knocked Clark forward, he couldn't help smiling. He was *part of a team.*

With *skills.*

Catherine-Lucille's Guide to Simple Stuffy Making

Okay, eyes front, people!

What, you think it's funny? That I know how to sew? Because I'm a *girl*? Let me tell *you* something, noob. My cousin who taught me makes his own jeans and he's studying to be a fashion designer in New York City and you're a sexist piece of work, so just SIT down and SHUT up and LISTEN.

I don't want to see ANYONE working on ANYTHING less than a six. You hear me? There's no point. You might as well give up, go home, and plunk your money down on some piece of trash beanbag toy or something stupid and big-eyed like that.

Now. This is a lot like making a zipper dangle, with a few differences.

1. It is larger.
2. You start with the cloth's *wrong* sides facing out. When you are done sewing, you turn the Stuffy *right* side out, stuff, and sew closed.
3. You use a running stitch.

READ THROUGH ALL THE INSTRUCTIONS FIRST!

Step 1
Designing and cutting out your Stuffy

Sketch out approximately how your Stuffy will look. Is it a creature with a big, soft
belly which is cut out of a
different piece of cloth? Does it
have spots? Long ears? Paws or
fins? You can have more detail
and finer appendages this time
because of the larger cloth and
different method of sewing. But
don't make it too complicated or
the appendages *too* too thin!

    Cut out the front and back of
the body, following the same instructions from the Zipper Dangle chapter. Make sure
you wind up with two mirror shapes that match up.

Step 2
Sewing your Stuffy, or: Welcome to the running stitch

Thread your needle and tie a
knot in the end (see above, again
in the Zipper Dangle chapter).

    With a larger stuffy, it
makes sense to either pin the
two pieces of cloth together, or
stick them together temporarily
with double-sided tape or
regular tape or whatever. You
want to make sure the pieces
of cloth don't slip or move as

you sew. REMEMBER: **RIGHT** OR **PRINTED** SIDES OF THE CLOTH FACE EACH OTHER ON THE INSIDE. Because you're going to turn the skin *right side out* to stuff it.

The running stitch:

- Push the needle up through both layers of cloth from the back. (Remember: You are turning the cloth right sides out when you are done so it doesn't really matter which side you start from.) Pull it gently but firmly until the knot slides up against the cloth.
- Put the needle *back* down through the two layers of cloth from the same side, about a half a centimeter from where the needle came out.
- Push the needle back up through the two layers of cloth, again, half a centimeter from where the needle came through last.

Repeat repeatedly! Keep doing this until you're all the way around and back, five centimeters or so from where you started. Then tie a knot up close to the cloth and clip the thread. MAKE SURE YOU LEAVE THAT GAP between the beginning and the end of your sewing for turning and stuffing.

Step 3
Stuff your Stuffy!

Carefully, using a blunt pencil or rounded end of a chopstick, turn your Stuffy right side out through the gap that you just left near the end/beginning of where you sewed (you did, right? I warned you *lots*).

Use the same blunt instrument (or your fingers) to stuff your Stuffy. DO NOT PUSH TOO HARD and do not use too much stuffing

Step 4
Finish sewing your Stuffy

Thread the needle and tie a knot
in the ends again.

Pushing your needle from
the back of your Stuffy, close the
gap you left open to stuff using a
whipstitch.

Tie a knot close to the cloth
and snip the threads.

Step 5
Detail time!

With a bigger Stuffy, you have way more room to play around! Puffy paint is great for
this. So are sequins and googly eyes. Fangs, teeth, intricate eyes, wings, tail ... You
can go back to using the whipstitch to sew on larger details out of other pieces of
cloth, like muzzles or bellies.

FIFTEEN

Day

The circles on his lunch sandwich were not the color of real meat. They were a watery pink, bright like bubblegum, but also a little see-through. None of the cooks seemed to be able to give a clear answer as to whether the meat was bologna or ham.

Anna's vegetarianism suddenly began to make a lot more sense.

Like everyone else, Clark filled up on as many chips as he could grab before the giant bowl on the table was depleted. Then he stuffed two of the tiny, hard green apples into his shirt for later and went looking for the witch viburnum.

It wasn't actually that hard; all the bushes around the edge of the pine grove but one were scruffy and starved for light. This one was lush and full, with giant, heart-shaped leaves, like it thrived on darkness. A perfect place to hide. He tiptoed around to the back and found a group of kids sitting there. They all looked quiet and serious, and Catherine was tracing things in the dust with a white beaver-chewed stick.

"Hey." She nodded at him and he settled into the dirt beside them.

From here he could see the forest amphitheater, the path to the lake, the entrance to the canteen, the awning of the offices. In other words, everything. Catherine-Lucille had staked out the perfect hidey place. She was a military genius.

"Everyone, this is Clark. Clark, this is Saneema, James, and Scooter."

"Welcome, shorty," the oldest camper—James—said with a smile. He was tall and could have been a counselor. "No one can overhear us here. There's no place for any*thing* to hide. You can say whatever you want. This is a totally safe space."

"So tell us, Private. What's your story?" Catherine-Lucille prodded.

Clark took a deep breath and told them about his dad, and the displaced and injured Stuffies, and the things he thought he saw.

... Which was utterly insane.

It was insane to be talking about Monsters and Stuffies and parents under the bright sunshine and friendly, leafy shadows. To people he didn't know.

But they listened intently and no one interrupted.

"Whoa," Scooter said when he was done.

"Your dad? Really?" Saneema demanded, looking to James

and Catherine-Lucille, hoping one of them would deny it. "But adults *can't* be attacked by Monsters."

"It's very rare," James said gravely. "But it does happen. Right, C. L.?"

"Yeah," Catherine-Lucille said, thinking about it, staring at the little marks that her stick made. They were all treating it as if it were real. They were asking all the right questions. It was unbelievable.

She took a deep breath. "I mean, it's possible—I don't know anyone it's happened to, personally. For a Monster to stalk an adult is super bad. Either there's something wrong with the adult, like *really* wrong, like it's a family thing and he inherited the Monster from *his* parents. Or it's a very, very powerful Monster."

Saneema's eyes widened. "Like what? You don't mean…"

"Like, a Level Ten or something?" James whispered.

"Maybe higher. Eleven or Twelve. A King, even," Catherine-Lucille said reluctantly.

"A King? Monster? They have those?" Clark squeaked.

She was going to make some sort of dumb joke, right? Like a pun? Like, "something something *rhymes-with-king*?" And then they would all laugh.

Right?

"They're the worst of the worst." Catherine-Lucille drew little ugly S's in the dust. Then she put fangs on one. "You said your dad had puncture wounds, right?"

"Well, I mean, my mom thought they were from bedbugs.…"

"The most powerful Monsters—the really rare ones—are big. And *dangerous.* Some have needle teeth. Round for sucking." She pointed at her picture. "But their bodies are sick. Sick like smoke. Like pollution. Like death."

In a very, very hazy way, her drawing did resemble what he had thought he had seen in his parents' bedroom. He shuddered. Like *death?*

"How do you know all this?" Clark asked softly.

"People talk. I listen. My cousins told me some." She shrugged. "You get a knack for it—telling what's the difference between baby stories and what's real Monster stories."

"It's her gift," Saneema said.

"Is your dad protected at all?" James asked. "While you're here?"

"I made him a little Stuffy—I was telling Catherine-Lucille about it before," Clark said eagerly, holding his fingers together to indicate the zippy's size. "It's small enough to carry with him all the time."

"Maybe he will, maybe he won't," Catherine-Lucille said ominously. "What else?"

"I told my sister to keep Stuffies hidden in my parents' bedroom for me. She promised she would."

Catherine gave him a hard look in the eye. "How old is she?"

"Sixteen."

"Does she know about Monsters? For real?"

"Yes." Then he thought about it. "Kind of? She sort of

believes in them? But...maybe less than she used to? I don't know...."

Saneema swore softly. James sighed.

Catherine-Lucille shook her head.

"That's no good, Private. You got to check up on her. Make sure she's actually doing it. She may love you and stuff and mean to do what you asked, but teenagers are different. She might... just... forget. No offense, James."

James laughed good-naturedly. "None taken. I know I'm a child at heart."

"How do I *check up on her*?" Clark asked. "Letters take at least two or three days!"

Everyone was quiet, thinking.

"The phone," Scooter suddenly said, looking up at the group.

Clark realized that the tiny kid under the fishing cap was a girl.

"We're not allowed to call off-campus except for extreme emergencies," he pointed out.

"No, she means the *secret* phone," Catherine-Lucille said in a low voice. "The counselors keep an illegal cell phone hidden far away from the main office. So they can call their girlfriends or boyfriends or whatever. That's a *great* idea. You need to find it and use it to call your sister."

"In the woods?" Clark swallowed. "Won't I get caught leaving camp?"

"We can cover for you," Saneema promised. "Scooter's cabin is near yours. She can spread the rumor that you're doing a special self-esteem orienteering session or something like that."

"Yeah," James said, getting excited. "We'll just make sure different counselors hear different things. If it's not on a clipboard, it's not in their brains. They're kind of like really dumb robots sometimes. But, you know, nice ones."

Clark was silent. While it felt good to suddenly have a whole group of friends behind him, the idea was still terrifying. Just go off? By himself? Off the property? To find an illegal phone? What if he was caught with it? What if he broke his leg in the woods? What if a Monster—a King—found him and ate him?

"Where *is* the phone?"

"I'll have an operative get you the exact location. It's in the woods beyond the archery range."

"Are there Monsters in the woods?"

Catherine-Lucille snorted. "Yeah, but they're very, very rare. Don't worry about it. Monsters prefer places that humans have been—and then abandoned. They don't do well in the wild. Like the way shadows stick to you? Creatures from the Dark Places stick to *us*."

Clark realized he would have to think about that more later. Inside, under bright lights.

"Well, all right, I'll have Foon with me, so..."

"Negatory, Private." Catherine-Lucille struck her stick down into the dirt. "You have to leave him behind. If, for some reason, the adults need to look for you and they find the contraband—your Stuffy, I mean—they'll think you haven't gone far. They know you wouldn't leave him behind. So, logically, you *have* to leave him."

Leave Foon? While he walked in the woods by himself? What would he hold?

"Okay, I guess." His voice cracked a little.

"Go after lunch tomorrow," Saneema suggested. "During Quiet Time. If anyone asks, we'll say that thing about your self-esteem project. Or that you're constipated or something."

"No...I feel like massive diarrhea is way more believable," James said thoughtfully.

"Oh yeah, that's *much* better. You're right. Diarrhea."

"What?!" Clark yelped.

Catherine-Lucille shrugged. "It happens at camp all the time. The food here is terrible. People are always spending a loooong time in the outhouses."

"Bu...er, gl..."

Clark opened his mouth, but nothing coherent came out. It was like his brain couldn't choose between the indignity of the excuse, the dangers of the task, or the questionable effectiveness of the plan.

But...

Dad.

The marks on his neck.

How he had walked into a wall.

"Will tomorrow be too late?" he finally managed to say, resignedly.

"Hope not, Private," Catherine-Lucille said, clapping him on the shoulder. "But it's not like we have a choice. The rest of the day is taken up with classes and color wars. You'd be missed."

"Plus there's s'more pie for dessert," Saneema chimed in.

"Oh yes," Scooter said gravely. "Nobody *ever* misses s'more pie night."

Clark returned to the day's routine, his secret quest weighing heavily in the back of his head.

In Mindful Arts they had to make an instrument out of whatever they found, which was primarily sticks and rocks. One very clever girl found that throwing dirt, hard, onto the porch of the Mindfulness Cabin made a fairly pleasing sound. Bird feathers didn't make any noise at all, so they stuck them in their hair. NOT that they were pretending to be Native Americans with culturally insensitive accessories, they promised their counselor and mindfulness guide. It just looked cool.

Clark cracked up watching the kids around him beat rocks together and throw dirt and dance around crazily. The dirt girl laughed, too, and soon they all were, and the guide was pleased.

The color wars were actually fun—and, more importantly, a good distraction for Clark's fevered mind. He even made third place in the obstacle course, earning Team Go, Go, Indigo three points.

On the four-hundred-yard relay someone passed the baton to Clark—and there was a piece of paper wrapped around it.

He unstuck the note and shoved it into his pocket, losing a few seconds. That night in his bunk he opened and read it (with Foon looking on). It was a basic map of the camp including some of the area surrounding it, west of the lake. Hand-drawn over the printed image were orienteering symbols, like a dot-to-dot leading to the finishing star.

Clark studied it under his blankets, and then studied it more, trying to commit all the points and features to memory. Long after lights-out he held the paper up to the bright whiteness of the full moon. No magic extra symbols were revealed, no silvery lettering, but the glow let him read it for a while longer.

He fell asleep thinking about his dad, and trees, and compasses.

SIXTEEN

Night

Foon opened his eyes a second time, called by the Moon.

He looked around slowly. The sleeping boys were still—as strangely frozen in the night as he and all the other Stuffies were during the day. Moonlight lingered where it couldn't possibly have reached, sparking faintly in drifts over supine bodies, blankets, fuzzy heads.

Foon regarded his own Boy, who didn't even seem to be breathing. He stuck out a worried, cautious paw—claws retracted—and felt Clark's cheek. It was warm. He was just... asleep? More than asleep. Something else. Waiting in dreams for the magic of the night to be conducted and over.

Foon wondered if his Boy learned things about the world while he slept, the same way the little Stuffy did during the day, soaking in through his human skin what happened and what was said around him.

He carefully pushed the covers aside and slipped down from the bed and onto the floor. He landed in a knit cloth clump, arms and legs akimbo, still unused to movement.

From his upside-down position he could see a few other Stuffies gently taking leave of *their* Boys, all more nimbly than he. They were silently sliding down sheets and landing gently upright when their feet touched the floor. Then in two wavy columns they marched happily into the moonlight.

Foon quickly picked himself up and followed.

Working together, tiny creatures—an elephant, a vampire, a rabbit—got a grip on the cabin door and tried to push. And so did Foon, who saw that help was needed. They shoved and muttered and used their combined weight and were soon out, tumbling into the pure, bright light of the Moon.

Foon watched with awe as even more Stuffies came marching out of other cabins, in lines neither neat nor ordered, but joyfully solemn. There were horses, dogs, cats, pigs, birds. There were pillows with ears and tails, beanbags with big eyes, and tiny action figures that glittered brightly under the starlight.

Foon had no idea where they were all going but he hurried along boldly as if he knew.

They scuttled, trotted, scurried, and swam through the pine needles to a grove of whispery dark trees lit by the loving Moon. No one hurried to the high human benches; they made their own little circle on the soft ground.

At the top of the circle sat a surprisingly large bear. How someone managed to sneak or beg or wheedle such a gigantic thing into camp was beyond Foon's stuffed head. The bear was a very soft shade of light blue. He wore a velvet jacket with things pinned to it that didn't look quite child-made. A brown ribbon circled his head. He nodded silently at each and every Stuffy who came and sat down.

When they were all seated and no more came, he spoke. His voice resonated powerfully through the woods.

"By the Grace of the Velveteen, let us come to order."

"By the Velveteen, let us begin," everyone except for Foon murmured back.

"We have been blessed with a new initiate tonight. A Boy has reached out and given the spark of life to one of our number." The bear nodded down at Foon, who jumped at the sudden attention. "Come here, little one."

Foon rose as well as his still-soft legs would allow and hobbled to kneel in front of the imposing figure.

The bear reached out a paw and put it on Foon's head, crushing his horns a little. But it didn't hurt; his touch was warm and comforting.

"Welcome. You have been chosen to join us: in the Dark and in the Light, in love and in cloth, in safety and in danger. You join us."

"You join us," the other Stuffies repeated.

"From the very first day the sun rose over the world, there have been shadows . . ."

"For where there is Light, there is always Dark," the Stuffies finished.

"And you, my brave little friend," the bear said, for the first time looking directly at Foon (with big, kindly eyes), "have a harder path than most."

"What mean you?" Foon asked. Harsh-sounding words. But he had never spoken aloud before; his tongue was thick with Stuffing and his mouth moved slowly. He felt that the bear would understand and not be upset by his lack of etiquette.

"Your Boy," the bear said. "I can see it in his dreams: His Family is haunted by something very old and very evil. Something that reaches back beyond, past the ones who came before. A Darkness that lives beyond normal years.

"You have in your House a King Derker, thick and bold, perhaps preparing to lay its eggs."

There were mutters and whispers and low whistles. Foon kept his eyes on the bear.

"How powerful, this Derker?"

"It has fed on an Adult. It is old, and sick, and powerful. I cannot know for certain without seeing it myself. But I do not imagine he is less than a thirteen or so."

The murmurs grew louder; there were exclamations of dismay and outrage. Foon swallowed and tried to keep his eyes steady, but something must have shown on his face.

The bear smiled kindly. "Little one, you are not alone. You have friends here as well as back at your home to aid you in your battle. If the path to victory was easy, we would all be living in the Light by now.

"You must save your Boy and his Family. That is why you are here. That is why we are all here. You must destroy the

Monster that has made its lair in his family's home and minds. Can you swear to me you will follow the path of Light, or die trying?"

"I will." Foon bowed his head.

"Good." The bear sighed and eased back on his haunches, as if the hard part was done. "I am sorry your first test will be so hard—we have little time to teach and train you as a proper warrior of the Light. Do you know the exact number and manner of guardians your Boy has already?"

Foon thought carefully. He had been in the House once, and only briefly. He hadn't been with the Boy for very long. It would be many years before he was old, experienced, and loved enough—like the bear—to be able to read dreams and sense his Boy's thoughts. He felt *something*, just not clearly.

"I don't know. I feel...a comfort in him. All I can say is that he is not alone."

"I see. Well, that is something. There will be other forms of help, for you, of course. The Ap-Lionses in the kitchen have traditionally lent a hand to our cause. Sometimes the Dust Bunnies choose to aid. Seek kinship where you can."

"I will," Foon promised.

"Then let us part, strengthened in friendship and love, prepared to go back and fight the Darkness."

The bear lifted his head and aimed his muzzle at the sky, his black eyes sparkling with the reflected light of the Moon.

He roared a mighty roar, a good sound, full of power and hope. In fading it became a chant, his voice falling and rising in mesmerizing and wordless cycles. Foon looked up at the sky around the bear, the stars, the beautiful depths of blue space. Other, older Stuffies joined in, humming or howling or singing the haunting melody.

Somehow they all knew to finish at the same time, drawing out the final note, the bear's voice going silent last.

He bowed his head.

"By the Grace of the Velveteen, go in peace."

"We go, with Love and Light," everyone responded, and Foon figured out to do it, too.

He rose and looked around the world with new appreciation. He wasn't alone. There were Stuffies everywhere, doing the same hard tasks as he. They all were part of something good—something great.

He would protect his Boy and Family. As they all did.

When the moonlight ebbed and he slipped back into the cabin and his boy's arms, Foon fell fast asleep, calm and sure of himself, ready for whatever came next.

SEVENTEEN

Day

Clark woke up with a cramp in his stomach. This would be the most illegal thing he had ever done in his entire life.

"Bye, Foon," he whispered, tucking his Stuffy back under the covers. "Sorry, but you gotta stay here and keep watch and pretend that everything is normal until I'm back."

From that moment time sped up and slowed down and stopped in fits and spurts.

Brushing his teeth seemed to take forever. He looked around nervously, but of course no one noticed anything. There wasn't any *thing* to notice. Then suddenly he was most of the way to the mess hall with no memory of the walk. Pokémon Thief shot him a sour look. Did he know? Was he going to rat out Clark to the counselors?

No. He was being ridiculous. No one knew his secret plans

except for Catherine-Lucille and her friends. No one could read his thoughts.

At breakfast he ate two helpings of cereal since he would be cutting out of lunch early. He was the last kid out, slurping the dregs from his bowl as he brought it to the dishwashing station. Time crawled again as he waited at the cold foggy beach for his canoeing partner, Jaylynn, to arrive. A newt almost surfaced in the black water near him, hanging there for a moment before swishing its tail and lazily finding a better depth. Clark shivered in sympathy—how could the little amphibian endure such cold?

Time passed faster once he was on the lake and faster still in the Crafts Cabin. He kept sewing into his thumb, causing little fairy-tale pinpricks of bright blood. His Project was a special protector Stuffy for his dad. He would be half horse, like Winkum, and half owl, like Snowy—both of whom Clark missed terribly despite Foon's comforting presence. James, who loved mythology, had suggested the word *hippokoukou*: the creature would be like a hippogryph but with an owl's head and wings instead of an eagle's. So Hedwig the Hippokoukou would have a big mane (no points), claws (one point), sharp beak (one point), and a scepter that could double as a spiked mace (one point). Clark thought about adding a manticore's tail, but figured that would be mixing things up too much.

Catherine-Lucille shot him a warning look every time he opened his mouth. He gave her a thumbs-up, knowing not to discuss anything about the Plan.

He bolted down his lunch, which was hard, because it was some sort of hot beef stew best reserved for long meals.

Or possibly dogs.

Then, with map in hand, he walked to the edge of the camp, as if he were visiting the nurse, and slipped into the woods.

The sun shone hard and yellow; the fields and beach would already be getting hot. But at the edge of the hardwood forest everything was soft golden and white: the snowy trunks of birch trees, last autumn's leftover yellow leaves dotting the ground. The bright lime leaves of this year made the air beneath the branches glow like his mom's green tea.

The quiet was amazing and absolute. Distant sounds of campers shrieking came to him as if in a dream. He could hear twigs snapping under the feet of tiny rodents, insects shifting positions, birds letting out a single tentative midday call.

He wasn't scared at all....

And that was strange.

Clark looked at his map.

The first orienteering symbol was a small black triangle, which meant *boulder*. He scanned the land around him: Against the bright trunks and moss he easily picked out the shape of a big gray rock. He hurried over to it, keeping his thumb on the map near the triangle to hold his place.

The next symbol was a stone wall, which was somewhere diagonally in front of him. He couldn't see it through the trees. He would need his compass to find the right angle and direction.

Clark stepped off the path, forward. The woods closed in behind him. He was disconnected entirely now: from the camp, from safety, from help.

But a stone wall meant that humans had been there at some point, right? Someone had to have built it, probably close to an old farm or something. So he couldn't really have been that deep into the woods. Because who the heck would put a stone wall in the middle of a forest, anyway? Sheep didn't graze on pine needles.

But when he finally found it, the stone wall turned out to be extremely creepy.

It was less a *wall* than a mostly straight pile of rubble, like the remains from some ancient, terrible war that had divided two realms. On his side was the bright birch and beech and maple forest. On the other were the pines, the same creepy gnarled gray ones that also ringed the lake. The ones here were taller, darker, infinite. Less like undead hands than pillars in a very scary temple from a very, very scary movie.

The next point on the map was somewhere on that side, among those trees.

Clark took one look back at the friendly woods, and the edge of the camp, which he imagined he could just barely see.

Was he really doing this? Him, Clark Smith, the good kid who never got into trouble and never did anything weird beyond carrying stuffed animals around?

He wished he had Foon with him. He wished he had finished the hippokoukou.

He wished...

And then he carefully stepped over the stone wall and into the shadows of the black trees.

Nothing happened.

It was definitely cooler in the shadows.

The needles crunched softly under his feet as he made for the last symbol, a bridge over a wavy stream. He clambered up the side of a small hill riddled with the roots of ancient pines that seemed to exist only to trip him.

Wait—was that poison ivy?

He panicked, trying to remember what his counselors told him. Vine on a tree, bright green and reddish... One, two, three, four, *five* leaves! Not three! Safe!

He took stock of his surroundings. The other side of the hill led down to a rounded depression at the base of several more tiny, sharp, pine-needle-covered hills. At the bottom of this was a shallow stream that ran silently over rocks and pebbles. Two logs were thrown across it, closely side by side.

Some bridge.

Clark tromped down and stood on it, feeling a little silly.

Where was the phone? It wasn't on the map. The bridge was the last point drawn on it—the end. The black water turned gold over glittery silt but revealed no secrets.

Clark looked around him: he was at the lowest point in the little valley. Should anyone—or any*thing*—decide it wanted to eat him for lunch, he had no escape.

What was that?

In that tree over there?

Something moved in the corner of his vision, something large and black that seemed to lumpily cling to a thick trunk. It fell, peeling off the bark—then caught itself in midair.

A woodpecker swooped silently down from the upper canopy and fluttered its wings delicately at the last minute to land on a lower branch.

Dummy, Clark scolded himself. Keep your cool.

But—what was that crunching noise? *Behind* him?

Clark twisted around slowly, his heart just about stopped. Part of him would have been relieved to see a counselor. Even if she yelled at him. Even if he got in trouble.

After a couple of panicked seconds of his seeing nothing, the crunching stopped.

Then it began again. To his *left* this time.

Clark whirled around.

He could hear his own breath, loud in his ears like a nightmare. If he screamed would anyone hear? Where would he run to? What if he got lost?

A head popped out of the leaves; a black eye glared at him.

It was a chipmunk, digging around in the ground and making far more noise than seemed possible for such a tiny thing.

Clark let out a ragged breath. Catherine-Lucille had specifically said that Monsters were rare in the forest because they liked places humans had built but abandoned. He was probably in more danger back at the stone wall. This "bridge" didn't look more than a few years old. It looked like it was built by counselors or older campers as part of a trail project.

Counselors...

Counselors! With *phones!*

Clark went back to the bank of the stream and looked around the abutment where the ends of the logs rested. Nothing, not even a rock large enough to hide something under. He dug through the leaves. Nothing. Grinding his teeth at the effort, he pushed the logs aside, one at a time, to see if anything was buried under them. Nothing.

He ran to the other side of the bridge and checked there. Again: nothing, nothing, nothing.

Frustrated, Clark went back to the middle of the bridge to take another look at the scene. *Think outside the box,* his mother would have said. But really he had to think *inside* the box: inside the box of a counselor's head. If he were a counselor terrified of getting found out for having an illegal phone, where would he hide it?

The last place anyone would look for a phone.

Which would be... *aha!*

Clark knelt on the logs, flinching at the damp, slimy wood now pressed against his knees. He plunged his hands into the icy water and began fishing around. All while trying not to imagine crayfish and stinging backswimmers and water-dwelling Monsters (were there such things?).

He wondered what he looked like from the woodpecker's

perspective, a tiny bright spot of purple splashing in the water like a raccoon.

His fingers brushed against something cool and slick.

It took all his resolve not to pull his hand away.

He forced himself to find edges, to feel and pursue the smooth, wet sides until he had purchase. The thing slipped out of his numbed hands twice before he finally managed to pull out what he found.

It was a clear vinyl dry bag. Like what the counselors kept snacks and maps in when they were canoeing.

And inside it was...

The phone.

Clark shook the remaining droplets off and carefully opened the bag. The phone inside was simple, small, and black, a flip phone with no extra features. How did they charge it, whoever hid it here? The battery was at half.

No matter, he wouldn't take up much of their precious bars. He wiped his hands on his pants and dialed.

Buzz...

Buzz...buzz...

Clark prayed for Anna to pick up and not ignore the unknown number.

"WHO IS THIS?" a voice demanded on the other end.

Never had he been so overjoyed to hear her cranky voice.

"It's me. Clark."

"What? Clark?" The voice softened. "How are you calling me? I thought there were no phones. Is there an emergency?"

"No, it's fine. I . . . It's a . . . It's someone's illegal phone I stole for a sec."

"You? What? *Stole?* Illegal? I'm impressed, little brother."

"Yeah, okay, listen. Have you been doing what you promised to do?"

". . . What?"

"Have you been hiding stuffed animals around Mom and Dad's room?"

Clark tried not to sound impatient. He failed. Now that he was on the phone with his sister, looking out at the forest with the hard plastic pressed to his ear, he was more afraid of time passing, and of being caught, than of Monsters.

"You're calling me on an illegal phone to ask me if I've been hiding stuffed animals around Mom and Dad's room?"

"You promised."

"I know, I did. I did . . ."

He could hear her huffing, maybe blowing the perfect bangs out of her face. He could also hear the apology in her voice, the admission that she had done wrong. But as nice as that apology was, it was also irrelevant. She had promised, she had obviously failed, and their dad was in trouble.

"I'm sorry. I *did* put them in their bedroom when we first got home from dropping you off. But then Mom found them and . . . other things are going on here, Clark. I'm sorry. It just got kind of lost . . . in the . . . other stuff."

"What other stuff?" What could be more important than her promise? She didn't even have a boyfriend, or boyfriend intentions, right at the moment. What could possibly have been going on that would have made her break her promise?

Suddenly he thought of something and his heart went cold. "Is Grandma okay?"

"No, she's . . . she's fine. The chemo . . . It's just all a little more complicated than I thought. Than anyone thought. It takes a lot of time. I drive her to the hospital now . . . and wait with her, and drive her home. She's so tired afterward . . . all the time now, really.

"Sometimes it's scary, you know? She forgets the things you told her, like, four times. I guess that's a normal side effect. It's just . . . weird. But no, Grandma is as okay as she can be."

That wasn't quite the answer Clark was expecting. She wasn't dying; she wasn't well. Anna sounded worn out. Was that taking care of Grandma, or was it the Monster feeding on *her* now, too?

"She just needs a lot of energy and time. And Dad's been acting . . . like, even weirder than usual. Maybe he's got Lyme disease, or—"

"*THAT'S WHAT THE STUFFIES ARE SUPPOSED TO FIX!*" Clark practically shouted in exasperation.

"What? Clark, are you mental? Like, he's acting *really* weird. Like sick. Like actually sick."

"Yes, I know. I know *why*," Clark said, stomping on the rickety log. Everything she said verified the ridiculous truth. Monsters were haunting his dad, and the moment he wasn't protected he fell under their power. "And we can fix it. Please trust me, Anna! I know what I'm doing."

Anna muttered something unintelligible, as if she were holding the phone away from her face.

"I know it sounds crazy," he pleaded. Each word felt like a betrayal, but he had to get her on his side. "The Stuffies really can protect him! Please! Just do it! It'll take, like, five seconds!"

A sigh. "Okay..."

"So you'll put the Stuffies back there?" he pressed.

"Yes, Clark, I will." She sounded tired. Not like Anna tired, not spent-all-night-viewing-the-moon-and-partying-with-her-friends tired, but real tired. Like *Dad* tired. "I promise. Really."

"Thank you," he breathed. "And tell Grandma I love her and I'll make her a lanyard in Crafts."

"You're a weird little kid, Clark. But I love you."

"I love you, too, Anna."

He closed the phone before he felt stupid about saying that.

Clark returned to camp without having to look at the map—which was good, because he was thinking about everything except where his feet were going.

On the one hand, Anna hadn't *kept* doing what he had asked, and what she had promised. She deployed the Stuffies maybe once and then forgot about it. And their dad got worse.

On the other hand...whether or not she believed him, she now realized how important this was to Clark. He could tell from the tone of her voice that she felt bad and really would try to fix her mistake.

He hopped over the stone wall, letting his hand brush along

the trunks of the birch trees. One bright green leaf grabbed his eye and he snapped it free.

And then he felt guilty, because it was a living part of the tree. So he stuck it behind his ear. Maybe he would write a letter to Anna on it. She loved weird stuff like that.

Back on the main campus Catherine-Lucille and another girl were playing tetherball.

She paused mid-hit to give him a questioning look.

He gave a micro-nod.

She gave him a thumbs-up.

Then she took the ball and whacked it like she was one of those Japanese anime heroes in a mechanized suit of armor: hard as sin, perfect aim, no grace at all. The other girl hit it back just as hard. Clark gave them both a salute and continued on.

A glow as warm as a campfire radiated from the pit of his stomach. He had snuck away from camp and not been caught. He had been given a quest and succeeded. He found a phone hidden in the middle of the woods like something out of a modern Narnia. And almost none of the campers around him knew about it. It was his special secret. And if Anna finally did what he asked—and maybe chose the bigger Stuffies—their dad would be okay at least until he got back and could fix things properly.

When he fell asleep that night he was utterly exhausted and content, even smiling a little.

EIGHTEEN

Night

The now-diminishing light of the waning Moon gave a certain urgency to the circle of friends. They were running out of time to talk and make merry, to pass on wisdom and tell old tales.

The bear summoned a blazing fire from the stars—each one a loving sun on its own. A doodlebird made music; a sloth banged on rocks that sounded out like wild drums. Stuffies danced around the flames, singing to the sky.

Foon approached slowly, almost timidly, until a beautiful saber-toothed tiger extended her paw.

"Come sit down, new brother! You have much to receive in our short time."

He accepted her invitation and sat crisscross-applesauce as best as his short hind legs would allow.

"I was just telling the big folk here about how we divvy up the work," came a loud little voice from down below on his left.

A shiny, long-bearded dwarven fellow in silver armor with numbers at his feet—not his real Stuffy stats—waved at him before turning back to the rest of the crowd. "My men and women..."

"And dragons!" came another tiny voice from someone else Foon couldn't see, farther to his left.

"And *dragons*," the fighter corrected with a bow. "We take out the cannon fodder, leaving the Higher Monsters to you big ones—the Silver Fish and whatnot. I go for the Feks in the corners, the dragon and her rider take out the Cowbers near the ceiling. Or Tahks, if we *have* to go to the basement, or the garage."

There were shudders all around at this.

Foon twitched his horns, feeling lost.

"Tahks have armor, and they scuttle low to the ground, often several at once," the saber-toothed tiger whispered, seeing his distress.

"Very easy to demolish their ranks," said a kindly old... well, Foon wasn't quite sure what it was. During his time in the grandmother's hands, becoming, he had absorbed much of the world. But not everything. This Stuffy was blue, had two large legs but no arms, and a row of pointy teeth. Unsettlingly like a Monster. "Good to practice on, for a newly made like yourself."

"There is so much. I don't know if I will learn enough before I return to my Boy's House and join the battle," Foon said, horns crimped with worry.

"You'll do your best. And we will help you," the saber-toothed tiger promised. She pointed toward the fire. "Listen: all of the songs teach. Look: all of the dances tell."

Foon turned to look. What he had taken for a joyful romp resolved itself into a mock battle. An elephant advanced, advanced, advanced; a robot flung out its arms with smooth precision, blocking her light blows. Then they spun and switched sides.

They were practicing battle moves!

"You have a few more nights here yet. Ask questions, dance, sing. We'll give all the answers we have." The blue thing patted Foon's hand with one of its sort-of-feet.

"Can you tell me more about the Ap-Lionses?" Foon asked politely.

"They have the hearts and honor of lions," the saber-tooth tiger said. "That's why they are named so. They cannot move as we do, but defend their Families as best they can."

"They have rules and etiquette all their own," the blue Stuffy added. "Which it wouldn't hurt for you to learn a bit of, if you're looking to make a good impression…"

As the older Stuffies spoke Foon gradually felt a giant weight ease off his soft shoulders. The Light wouldn't let him go off on his journey unschooled in the ways of the world and Monsters. Everyone here understood and would help him prepare for his task.

He listened and watched the fire and the bright sky above and his spirits lifted.

All he could do was try.

That was all anyone—the universe, the Moon, his Boy—expected.

NINETEEN

Days

On the lake, Clark and his partner finally got their act together. When they paddled they did so effortlessly and simultaneously. Clark could see when Jaylynn's arm started its upward movement; she could somehow feel when he dipped his oar into the water. They wound up having to wait around for the other canoers to get themselves in the right direction, to sync their own paddling and push ahead.

They used this time to discuss BB-8 and R2-D2 and blasters versus bowcasters.

They debated *Rogue One* and whether it belonged with the rest of the movies.

And on the whispered count of three when the counselor wasn't looking they "accidentally" brought their paddles down flat on the surface of the lake, causing a clear sheet of water to explode out and soak the other campers.

In Orienteering, Clark asked what the additional symbols in their pamphlets were since they looked like the ones on his secret map. He started coming in first or second on their drills, and when they drew up teams for the next color war, everyone wanted him on their side.

In Crafts, Catherine-Lucille helped him with the trickier bits of his hippokoukou: the thin running stitches that his beak required, the innovation of slicing scissor-slits along his neck-ruff to make it look and move more like real fur.

He watched the illegal games of Pokémon and Magic that happened—sometimes with hand-drawn cards—late at night, after lights out. Pokémon Thief no longer bothered him, or even gave him a dirty look.

Breakfast, lunch, dinner, and snacks were, of course, all disgusting. Something strange was happening, Clark realized.

Camp...wasn't...actually...that bad.

Would it be better to be home in the backyard, reading or playing?

Absolutely.

Definitely.

Yes.

Of course, then he wouldn't be canoeing.

Or swimming.

Or going on a treasure hunt in the trees like a great fantasy quest.

Or talking to anyone about Star Wars.

(Anna allowed him exactly forty-five minutes of Star Wars–related discussion every two weeks. She tried her best to pay attention during those forty-five minutes, but it was barely enough time to get everything out.)

So…maybe?

On a whim, even though he didn't *like* like her, Clark made Pony Girl a quick feltie zipper dangle: a purple idea of a horse with a rainbow mane and tail colored in with marker, a powerful lightning bolt on its butt.

Pony Girl's eyes went bright and wet and red. She flung her arms around him and then ran off, clutching it tightly.

"Hm. Not bad, Private," Catherine-Lucille said.

No one made fun of him and Pony Girl anymore—at least not seriously. People actively wanted to be his friend. They saw him talking with Catherine-Lucille, playing tetherball with Scooter, bumping knuckles with James.

Or maybe it was because of the way he walked now, especially after his illicit phone call to Anna. Confident. Carefree. *Jaunty.*

Maybe it was how the box of brownies that Anna had sent were quickly confiscated by the counselors—despite the sneaky TOTALLY GOOD-FOR-YOU BOOKS ABOUT CAMPING AND OTHER WHOLESOME & HEALTHY EDUCATIONAL STUFF label on the package.

"Aww, that's the *worst*," everyone in Sunfish Cabin moaned, cookie paradise snatched so rudely out of their mouths and tummies. Somehow Clark came out looking even better than if he had actually managed to share the treats.

By the time Saturday morning rolled around, Clark wasn't *eager* to stay at camp, exactly, but he wasn't as desperate to leave as he thought he would be. He bought a camp hat and a Sharpie with his remaining canteen money and had everyone sign it: Backward-Baseball-Cap Boy (Shawn), Pony Girl (Grace), James, Scooter, Catherine-Lucille, Saneema, Jaylynn, and everyone else, including his cabin counselor.

"Can I get your e-mail address?" he asked Catherine-Lucille formally, holding out his journal.

"E-mail? Who uses e-mail?" She rolled her eyes and scrawled a number next to her initials.

He felt different than he had a week ago under the bright Sunday morning sun, giving high-fives and this time *bouncing* over to the amphitheater. He looked around eagerly for his family in the happy crowd of campers grabbing and hugging their moms and dads and brothers and sisters—but he couldn't find the Smiths.

Finally he saw his mom, standing alone.

"Mom!" He ran forward and threw his arms around her.

"Clark!" She smiled and hugged him close, lifting him up onto his toes like she did when he was younger. She smelled like soap and the half-fancy perfume she wore on special, but not *super* special occasions.

"Where's Dad and Anna?"

"Your dad, uh, he's really not feeling well," Mrs. Smith said reluctantly. "Didn't think he could make the car trip. He's at home, in bed. He's really sorry he couldn't come."

"Oh." Clark was confused, and then worried. What about Anna and her promise? What about the Stuffies? Weren't they protecting him? "Where's Anna?"

"She's checking in on your grandmother. Grandma Machen isn't eating as much as she should. She needed some extra help today. Let's get your stuff and get out of here and go home and see them!"

She smiled like the sun, and Clark got caught up in her enthusiasm and grabbed his bag. His mom noticed Foon sticking out the top of his daypack—head out so he could look around—but *she didn't say anything.*

Clark talked most of the way home. He had so much to tell her! Mrs. Smith had her little earpiece in but didn't twiddle with it at all. Not even at red lights. It wasn't even on. When they stopped to get gas, she let him get a blue slushy and then sit in the front seat. The first sip was the best, most magical taste in the world, like bubblegum ice and lollipop and melted Popsicle. It made his tongue go funny when he tried to talk.

But it didn't stop him.

"Wow. It all sounds . . . even better than I thought it would," Mrs. Smith said.

"I want to go back to camp next year," Clark said before he could stop himself. But upon pausing—and letting some of the slushy dribble down the back of his throat—he realized it was true. "But I want to go the same week D. A. does. And Catherine-Lucille."

"I'm sure we can arrange that. Did...anyone notice your... stuffed animal?"

Clark shrugged. "A few other kids brought them. And Catherine-Lucille likes them and everyone's afraid of her. And we made some in Crafts. Look! I made this for Dad!"

He carefully pushed Foon aside and took out the hippokoukou, now finished with a fluffy silver-and-white neck ruff and white wings. Not quite a tank, but maybe it would do...

"Oh wow, Clark." His mother did a double take when she saw it. "*You* made that? That's...incredible! It looks like it's from a store."

"It's better," Clark said, without elaborating why. Plus two for handmade, plus two for love.

"It *is* better. So Catherine-Lucille. Is she a friend of yours? Did you make any other friends?"

"Oh yeah. Jaylynn and Saneema and James and Scooter. We all traded e-mails, but I got C. L.'s phone number, we're going to text. Can I use your phone sometime? Or maybe we can set up my computer to do it? Or maybe it's time to get my own phone, like Anna?"

"Slow down, Clark Kent," his mom said with a smile. "You get a girl's number and suddenly you're all grown up."

"MOM!" He knew she was joking, mostly, but that didn't stop the redness from prickling his face. "It's not like that!"

"All right, all right, I was kidding...."

Clark rolled his eyes and looked out the window, imagining a world where he and his new friends could hang out all the time, by phone and video and in real life, and the sky was always as blue as it was out the car window.

TWENTY

Day

As they pulled into the driveway of their neat little home, Clark opened the door and leaned out, sucking everything into his eyes. Did it look different? Somehow he thought it would. But the house, the yard, the well-trimmed bushes, looked *exactly* the same. As if a week hadn't passed. As if Clark hadn't spent seven days away from his family and subsisted on terrible food and become an adventurer and made his own Stuffy.

"Hey, c'mon, Clark, this bag isn't going to carry itself," Mrs. Smith said, interrupting his thoughts. Clark trotted around to the back of the car and threw the duffel over his shoulder, practically bending in two from the weight of his dirty clothes. Then he fished around in the daypack until he found his new Camp I Can hat and stuck it jauntily on his head. Making sure Foon was positioned so he could get his first *real* look at his new forever home, Clark finally felt ready to go in.

"I'm home!" he called, throwing open the door.

Inside was silence.

Inside, bright day was weakened as soon as it filtered through the manmade windows and door cracks.

It *did* smell funny, Clark realized, taking a big sniff of what should have been familiar scents of home. The air conditioner was running full blast despite it not being a terribly hot day.

Clark realized he was hesitating, holding back from going in.

Then his pack shifted and Foon's head whacked against his shoulder.

"Right," Clark said. "I've got you, you've got my back."

He squared his shoulders and stepped over the threshold.

"Dad? Dad? I'm home...."

He dropped his duffel on the floor right next to the pile of shoes and went running up the stairs.

"CLARK! WASH YOUR HANDS!" his mother shouted. "AND WE NEED TO DO A LICE CHECK. AND DON'T TOUCH YOUR DAD UNTIL YOU'VE WASHED YOUR HANDS."

Clark got to the doorway of his parents' room...and stopped.

His dad was lying on the bed fully dressed, pale and sweaty. The shades were drawn. And even though the room was neat, the way Mrs. Smith liked it, there was something...*off* about it. Shadows seemed to have built up in the corners, where in other houses there would have been piles of dust. Surely those weren't cobwebs on the ceiling? Cracks in the paint? When had the paint cracked?

"Dad…?"

Mr. Smith's eyes rolled toward his son; otherwise his body and head didn't move at all.

"Clark…Mmmf. Good to see mmmf. Camp mmmf?"

"Dad, are you okay?" Clark whispered.

He drifted in, drawn to his dad despite the terror the room exuded. As he drew closer he saw there were little black-and-red marks on his father's skin, mostly covered by the collared button-down shirt he had decided to wear in bed. Old blood, fresh wounds.

And his mom was worried about *Clark* touching his dad?

"Just a little. Mmmf. Sick. Summer cold," his dad said, try-ing to sound chipper. But then his eyes fluttered shut, and he seemed to drift off.

"I made something, Dad," Clark said softly, pulling out Hedwig.

His dad didn't respond.

Clark slumped. He had spent a *lot* of time getting the seams just right, picking them out and resewing them again and again under Catherine-Lucille's perfectionist eye.

But, he reminded himself, that wasn't really the point of the Stuffy.

"Here, Dad." He carefully laid the little hippokoukou on the pillow next to his father's head. Despite the grim and gray-ness of the room, or perhaps because of it, his fur seemed to almost glow. A healthy orange, of summer sunsets and orange juice and fancy beach stones.

Mr. Smith's eyes stopped fluttering beneath their lids. He sighed one big, solid breath and fell deeper asleep. His face relaxed.

Relieved, Clark quietly backed out of the room, looking around for the Stuffies that were supposed to be hidden there.

None. Not a one.

There was a single token of Anna's presence: a charm from her bag, a shiny, trashy vampire emoji smiley face made out of cheap metal. It hung out of sight, clipped to the bottom of the quilt. Practically useless.

A car pulled up in the driveway, a very familiar-sounding car. But when Clark turned with relief to meet his grandmother, only Anna came up the stairs.

"Welcome home, intrepid camper!" But she was distracted and her smile was tired.

"Is Grandma in the car? Is she coming in?" he asked excitedly.

"No, she's at home, resting. I'm using her car to take care of her while she's sick. Nice hat."

"I thought it wasn't a big deal," Clark said, his voice rising. "Mom said. It was like a baby cancer. Grandma was going to be fine."

"Grandma is totally going to be fine," Anna said firmly, in a tone Clark rarely heard her use. A *grown-up* voice. "But it's still cancer, Clark. Well, actually it's the chemo that makes her sick and weak. She sleeps a lot. Sometimes I just sit and watch TV with her. Maybe you could do that now, too?"

That last statement had a little bit of a spank in it.

Irritated, Clark shook the vampire charm. "What about what you promised to do? What about taking care of *Dad*?"

Anna let out an impatient breath, blowing her less-perfect-than-usual bangs into a little puff. "Yeah, sorry, there's other things going on, right? I tried. I left that thing there." She took the charm back as if it were worth a lot and had pained her greatly to part with it, even for a moment.

Somewhere under Clark's anger he knew it meant a great deal to her. It wasn't a Stuffy, but it was something else important, something that represented a part of who she was. The fact that she left it there meant she was trying.

But...

"But it's not even a *Stuffy*," Clark found himself saying despite the more mature thoughts forming in his head. "Why didn't you use any of mine, like I asked? Can't you see how sick Dad is?"

"How sick *Dad* is?" Anna asked in disbelief.

"You *promised*," Clark whispered.

Anna bit her lip, as if trying to work out what to say.

"There were also...mitigating circumstances," she finally muttered.

"Like what?"

"Like lack of ammunition."

"Lack of what?"

Before Clark could question her further, Mrs. Smith came up the stairs. "See your room yet?" she asked.

What now? What was going on with his room?

Clark's head was swirling. Too much was happening too quickly.

"I'm sorry," Anna said cryptically, slipping away before he could ask her about *what*. It didn't sound like it was an apology for screwing up with the Stuffies. It sounded like it was for something else.

Clark approached his room warily.

There were better smells coming from it than from the rest of the house. Fresh paint and air from somewhere beyond the air conditioner.

He flipped on the light.

His bedroom had been completely redone!

The old worn rug had been replaced by a new one, thick and comfy. The walls were now his favorite color (deep blue). One was entirely taken up by a photomural of outer space. Which was a little weird, because it wasn't Clark's absolute favorite thing like it was with some kids. A castle or a view of Endor maybe would have been better. But it was still *amazingly cool*. He'd be able to lie in bed and pretend he was traveling through the stars to other planets.

His old, often-repainted bookshelves and cabinets had been replaced by a new set of shelves that covered an entire wall. All of his toys, books, puzzles and games had been neatly organized and stacked in labeled places. There were translucent bins on wheels for his Legos that he could easily pull out and put back. There was a built-in desk with a light that was shaped like the space shuttle.

From the middle of the ceiling hung a mobile of the planets. Saturn's rings sparkled with gold glitter.

His bed was the same, but the sheets and blankets were all new, and the coverlet was printed with what looked like glow-in-the-dark stars.

Snowy perched triumphantly on his pillow.

But that was it.

"Where are my stuffed animals?" Clark demanded.

"Don't you like your room?" His mom strode into the center of it and looked around proudly. "There are glow-in-the-dark stars on the ceiling, too, but you can't see them. They're almost the same color as the paint, during the day."

"Mom. My stuffed animals. Where are they?"

Clark began to get very, very angry. This obviously was all part of the plan. Get him away to camp for a week. Redo his room as a "surprise." *Get rid of all of his stuffed animals.*

And what about the other kids at camp? Did they come home to find their action figures confiscated? Their ponies? Their Pokémon cards?

"Clark, I put a lot of effort into this," his mom said through gritted teeth. "I would appreciate a little . . . appreciation."

"*MOM!* You got rid of all of my stuffed animals!" He had to bite back an "I don't care about your stupid new room." He *did* care. And it wasn't a stupid room. It was amazing. But . . .

"I didn't get rid of them," Mrs. Smith said with a disappointed sigh. "*We* didn't get rid of them. Your father and I thought you were making some pretty big grown-up steps, going to camp, going into fifth grade next year, and thought you would like to try a more grown-up way of living."

Clark was pretty sure most grown-ups didn't have a photomural of distant galaxies on their bedroom walls or lights shaped like rocket ships, but this didn't seem like a useful point to bring up just then.

"Where are they?"

"They're ... put away."

"Bring them back!"

His mom sighed again. She put her hands on his shoulders.

"Why don't you just try it? For one night. Maybe two. Just try it. I think you'll find it's much more comfortable not sleeping covered in all of that fake fur."

"I don't want to try it," Clark said. "I want them back."

"Well, you're *going* to try it," his mom snapped. "We'll revisit this discussion tomorrow."

She walked purposefully out of the room, trying not to look defeated.

Clark was full of feelings.

No wonder his dad was so sick, with no Stuffies to protect him! Anna really *had* tried. She probably *had* put the Stuffies around the room, hidden them, when there were still Stuffies to hide. But when they were all confiscated she had nothing to work with.

That was also the reason for her weird apology, Clark

realized. He knew his sister; she must have fought with their mom when the Stuffies were confiscated. She had also probably tried to stop it.

Okay, so she *did* take off like a deserter so she wouldn't have to see him discover what had happened to his Stuffies. But that was kind of understandable. It was an uncomfortable moment.

But why didn't she bother looking for the missing stuffed animals? Or substitute any of her own?

Maybe she was too distracted or tired if she was spending all of her time with Grandma Machen.

Clark felt a little spike of guilt. He would have to apologize back later.

And he would go visit Grandma Machen and spend time with her, even if it meant playing Scrabble, which she loved and he hated.

But for now . . . there was Dad to worry about.

When had he last talked to Anna by the illicit phone? Four days ago? So the Stuffies had to have been removed after that. His dad had been unprotected for at least four full nights. And meanwhile there was a Level Eleven or Twelve King Monster lurking around the house, draining him dry. And maybe his sister, too, from her looks. Mrs. Smith also seemed a little tired, but that was probably from her work and taking care of his dad and all the effort that went into Clark's room.

Unless, of course, the Monster was getting her, too.

Clark shivered. He sank down on his bed.

It really was a nice room.

But without his stuffed animals, it wasn't home.

And it wasn't safe.

TWENTY-ONE
Night

Hedwig the Hippokoukou lay on the pillow next to his dad's head.

Anna had Siouxsie the Bunny and Fat Bob the pillow rock star and her vampire girls and weird little voodoo doll on *her* bed.

(Not, as Clark privately thought, the best companions for guaranteed loyalty. But the vampire dolls were at least a five—base three plus one for the fangs, plus one for the wings—and the voodoo doll a three and a half—base three plus a half for *sustainably imagined* magic.)

So maybe she would be all right.

Mrs. Smith wasn't asleep, of course; she was puttering somewhere in the bedroom, sorting shoes maybe.

Maybe that's why the Monsters didn't get her.

Maybe they couldn't outlast her.

Clark definitely couldn't. He was exhausted. In an attempt to distract him from thinking about or hunting for his lost Stuffies, Mrs. Smith had run the family ragged. She took them out for dinner to celebrate Clark's return, then stopped for ice cream, and then added on an hour at the skeeball arcade.

Mr. Smith stayed at home by himself, of course, which only made the whole thing worse.

Clark was worn from the inside out.

He hugged Foon tightly to his chest. Snowy would have been better for hugs; she was fatter, with thicker fur. But she was guarding Clark's back, faced away, toward the wall and the closet.

Terrible thoughts wrestled each other in Clark's head. Monsters he could only imagine, terrors he couldn't actually see. The fear of losing his father. The fear of losing his grandmother.

There was really only one thing to do, and it too was terrible.

But heroes always had to make hard choices.

Clark took a deep breath and sat up. He pulled Foon and Snowy out from under the covers and placed them in front of him.

"Listen," he said, voice cracking a little. "I don't know how this works. Sometimes...I don't know if this really works at all. But if you can hear me, please listen. My dad is being slowly *eaten*"— he stumbled over the word—"by a Monster. He's being drained. He's all sick and awful. And everything I've tried to do hasn't worked. I need...I need you guys to find my other

Stuffies. Can you do that? I mean, I'll look for them first thing tomorrow. But I'm worried about tonight. Dad's got Hedwig the Hippokoukou, so he might be okay, but Mom might move him."

Clark took another deep breath, trying to stop the little shudders that were threatening to silence him completely.

"I'll be okay. For one night. I went into the woods and got the phone by myself—I can manage. You guys need to leave. You need to find everyone else and together kill the Monster. It's the only way to save Dad. *Please.* I know the Monster is supposed to be very strong, but with all of you working together it should be fine."

He squeezed Foon. "I know this is super hard, and crazy, your first night back. But . . . if I made it into the woods and back at camp, you can do this. I know you can.

"And I'll be fine. I'll stay under the covers. I'll put a pillow over my head. Just . . . save Dad. Please?"

Foon's button eyes remained buttons. Snowy's eyes glittered, but that was just from unseen lights reflecting on the shiny plastic.

"Okay. Thank you," Clark said, kissing them each on the head. Was that weird? He didn't care.

And then he carefully set them next to each other, at the end of his bed, facing away from him, toward the door.

Alone and shivering, Clark pulled the covers up over his head and prayed for morning to come quickly.

TWENTY-TWO
Night

Foon opened his mismatched button eyes.

He had to find the other Stuffies! They had to kill the King Derker!

He looked around, confused at first by the intensity of these ideas that did not entirely originate in him. His paws twisted on his spear. His lanky horns twisted in the thick night air.

There.

Way at the other end of the bed, where Foon should have been as well: his Boy, dreaming in a fitful, fevered sleep. *That* was where his orders came from. A hazy day-memory of sitting, listening as the Boy begged him to go.

Next to Foon was the only other Stuffy in the Room.

"Snow Killer," he said. "I am Foon. Are you risen?"

"I am always risen, guarding my Boy," the snow owl replied regally—but not unkindly. "Welcome, newcomer."

"Where are the others? When I was first brought here I had thought there were many...but now they are gone?"

The owl breathed a sound that was somewhere between a sigh and a growl. She eased herself into proper standing position, flexing her furry toes as she found a good purchase on the blankets.

"All the others were taken. In one blow. It was a catastrophe, an utter routing. I was left alone to defend until the Boy's return, a difficult job. Other Monsters tried to claim the bedroom, emboldened by the presence of the King Derker that infects this House."

The owl turned her head all the way around so Foon could get a look at the back of her neck: an ugly pink rip gleamed in the darkness, and a tiny bit of Stuffing peeked out. Foon tried to imagine what could have possibly landed the blow on such a deadly creature.

"I do not believe our comrades are gone from the House," she continued speculatively. "I *feel* they are still somewhere. Imprisoned. The few Dust Bunnies I have managed to speak to have confirmed that there has been no...evidence of destruction, no Stuffing in the trash."

Foon contemplated this. Maybe it was good news.

The owl lowered her voice. "I believe they are held in the basement."

Foon remembered the shudders of his brethren from the Circle of Fire when basements were mentioned. But he didn't say anything; as this was his first real night, he didn't want to appear cowardly in front of his new comrade.

"It is almost as if the whole thing were planned. . . ." The owl did a funny thing with her shoulders, scootching down to look Foon in the eye with her own slit golden ones. "The King Derker is getting ready to lay its eggs. This would be a perfect opportunity for it to hatch them, unopposed, with everyone gone."

Foon's button eyes widened.

"It's all true, then."

"I fear it is so," the owl said grimly. "No longer content to squirm and slither through the midnight passages of this sad House, the Monster now begins its attack before the Moon has even set on certain foul nights. And it takes more and more each time.

"The Father is unable to fight off the fell beast any longer. Now it's only a matter of time before the Monster claims him entirely and moves into his skin."

"Into . . . into the body of a Grownedup?" Foon protested.

"It is very, very rare," the owl said gravely. "Usually it is a child who is taken and then grows into adulthood, more Monster than human. There are forces involved here we cannot begin to fathom."

Foon gripped his spear tightly, anger coursing through his fiber. "We must stop him!"

"Truly. Having a King Derker wearing the form of an Adult human would be a huge victory for the Dark—who knows what evil it would wreak?"

"We cannot both go, as the Boy wants."

"Absolutely not," the owl agreed. "He is very brave, our Boy, wishing to send us both to save his father. I sense a wonderful change in him; he is becoming stout-hearted and wise. But it would be folly to leave the Boy alone."

"Stay here and guard him well," Foon said. "I will go rescue the other Stuffies. Together we will all return and kill the King Derker and free this House of its Darkness."

"Excellent," the owl said, nodding. "I am pleased you are up to the task so soon. Time is short, I fear."

"And the night is Dark," Foon recited.

The owl snapped her beak and cried.

It was a terrifying call, the triumph of a predator. She threw open her wings and gave several mighty claps with them.

Foon was very impressed. He wished they could have gone together. Snowy would have been a stalwart companion indeed, perhaps even allowing Foon to ride on her back above such dangers as the floors presented.

"By the Grace of the Velveteen, I shall set off at once," he said, saluting her with his spear.

"By the Grace of the Velveteen, go then, hastily, and return victorious."

The owl bowed to him, wingtip touching her brow.

Foon slipped over the side of the bed, down to the floor, and began his journey.

TWENTY-THREE
Foon's Journey Part I

The floor of the Room was large and flat and featureless.

Foon regarded it nervously. Stuffies always preferred the tactically advantageous higher ground: beds, chairs, sofas, piles of clothes, and piles of other Stuffies. The mountain of a bed was behind him and the rug stretched out endlessly in front with nothing between it and the door.

He paused on his soft tippy-toes, turning this way and that, keeping his button eyes wide, unwilling to miss a thing. He gripped his spear with both short arms, ready for a surprise attack. His fiber heart beat loudly within his chest of rags.

But there was nothing—only silence.

Using the tip of the spear, he carefully lifted up one edge of the bed skirt that fell to the floor. There were no Monsters, of course. Snowy had done a magnificent job on her own. But there were also no Dust Bunnies. Not even a single baby Dust Pug. It was like they had been wiped out, or moved on after some great calamity had overcome the Room. Perhaps it was whatever had claimed the Stuffies.

Disappointing. Foon was hoping for at least a chat, and possibly a warning or word of advice.

He let the bed skirt fall back down. Nothing to do but move on.

The ceiling was so far away it might have been the sky. Cowbers could have been clinging in the corners, feathering the seams. But that was unlikely given Snowy and her wings. She would have made short work of them. And even if there were one or two new ones that night, they were of no import. With a combined Defense of one they wouldn't dare drift down to bother Foon. At worst they would titter and whisper about him in their ugly, unintelligible shadow language—while staying far out of the reach of his spear.

Still.

He wanted to walk backward the whole way to the door, keeping one eye on the air above him and another on everything else. He didn't like having the window and the closet behind him, even knowing Snowy was there. He didn't like being so newly made. Although he strengthened with every moment that passed, his soft legs sometimes still betrayed him, threatening to collapse.

Every nine steps he stopped and slowly made a big show of looking around. *I know you're there, Monsters,* he said through his soft, silent movements. *I know you can come through. I'm ready.*

Foon wasn't fearless.

He wanted very much to crawl back into bed with his Boy, snuggle under the covers. Courage was *not* doing that; courage was choosing to rescue and fight—even while afraid. *Especially* while afraid. Those who went into battle fearless were witless as well, and put their comrades into danger.

Many long moments later he reached the end of the rug. The door was properly *un*shut; the Boy was canny despite the severity of the situation. Foon put his paw on it.

He took one last look back at the giant bed. He could just make out a figure perched there, watching. Did she put a wing to her head, saluting him again?

Foon gestured back with his spear. Then he pushed the door and went through.

TWENTY-FOUR
Foon's Journey Part II

The vast hallway stretched out before him. Walls rose dramatically on either side, disappearing into the lofty height of the ceiling. A door was to his immediate left. Foon somehow knew or remembered from day-dreams that the Sister slept there.

It was too dark to clearly make out anything in that Room beyond the large black sleeping Sister shape on the far side of the bed. There were some smaller shapes around her that *could* have been Stuffies. Foon wondered. He could feel no Monsters there. Maybe he would find friendly comrades to recruit for his quest?

He took one tentative step toward the threshold—

And was rewarded by an angry hiss.

Somewhere on the bed, eyes or teeth glistening in what little light there was, a Doll sat up. An unfriendly, territorial one.

Foon stepped back quickly. He would get no help here.

But at least the Sister was protected. And this Room, while

not friendly, was at least safe. No Monsters would come near such a nasty and feral thing.

The next door was shut tight,

There was no doubt at all that behind it was the lair of the King Derker.

Seeping out from under the door was thick, fetid air redolent of Monster spoor. Something unspeakable had been festering and nesting in there. No puff of fresh breeze, no sun or moonlight, no army of Stuffies had breathed any life into that Room for a long time. The atmosphere itself had rotted.

Foon shivered. Whatever lived in there was bold enough and strong enough to feed on an Adult. The little Stuffy was glad he would not be coming back alone. Only with a small army would he be able to defeat it.

He turned back down the hallway. Beyond the Parents' Room the atmosphere seemed to grow hazy, as if the King Derker's foul miasma had leaked out of the bedroom and filled the space beyond, creating its own rank weather. The ceiling and even the walls were gradually erased in a gray fog. It was hard seeing anything more than a few Foon-feet ahead of him.

And then he saw *them.*

Huge. Ugly. Armless, legless, finless, gill-less. Swimming silently in and out of drifts of smog like snakes of the deep. Long slit mouths went most of the length of their body. These opened and shut continuously, revealing rows and rows of uneven, mismatched teeth. Human-looking teeth: flat and ivory, white and knobbed, tiny and bloody.

Foon held his spear tightly in his right paw. The saber-toothed tiger from the Circle of Fire had said that though they were large and frightening in appearance, Silver Fish were cowards and often skittish. Their attacks were vicious, and they had a Defense of six.

"Begone!" Foon cried out. "Leave this House now or face me and my weapon!"

One of the Silver Fish, turning toward him as noiselessly and suddenly as an eel, cracked its ugly mouth into a hideous smile that nearly split the thing in two.

"Stupid, foolish little toy," it rasped. "Newcomer. You have no power here. This House is under the control of a new Master now."

"No longer!" Foon declared, trying to keep the fear out of his words. "One more chance, Beast of Darkness. Leave before I cut out your blasphemous tongue."

The Monster opened up its mouth wide, wide, and wider still: as if to suck up all the air in the great hall, as if to spit out a thousand poisons, as if to deliver a final, scathing insult.

A tiny tongue, no more than a skinny root, waggled nastily at him.

Foon took his spear and hurled it.

He didn't bother with the creature's venomous eyes or slimy silver belly: He aimed directly down the thing's throat.

It screamed as the spear hit.

Waves of piercing, terrible sound ripped through the Dark

and the Light and echoed madly off the yellow walls of the House.

The thing exploded in a silent, ugly burst. Gray asymmetrical shards flurried to the floor. They disappeared when they hit the wood like the shadows of snowflakes.

Foon dove, managing to catch his spear before it, too, hit the ground.

The other Silver Fish paused their endless gliding and looping.

"Who's next?" Foon cried.

He circled the hall, shaking his spear above his head. The Silver Fish drifted above him warily.

The faintest wisp of air movement touched the back of Foon's argyle neck.

He whirled around.

One had come up silently behind him. Its jaw was unhinged, dangling like a giant scoop, ready to grab the little Stuffy.

SNAP!

A split second before the Monster smashed its ugly teeth together again—with Foon inside—the little Stuffy threw himself flat against the floor.

The Silver Fish quickly angled away to try another attack. Without looking, Foon stuck his spear back behind him and up—hard.

It impaled the Monster precisely through its throat.

Foon then caught the head of the Monster on the tips of

his horns and drove it down, pinning it against the floor. He pulled out his spear and thrust it into the thing's heart—or what passed for its heart. It died immediately, melting into nothing.

Like a school of something much more social and fishlike, the remaining Silver Fish turned tail and scooted away into the ugly haze.

The fog slowly rolled back, dissipating into the shadows.

Foon panted and leaned on his spear for a moment. His first real battle. Against *two* Defense Six Monsters!

In a different House, that might have been the end of it—for the night, at least. Rarely was a Family burdened with such a terrible infestation that epic battles needed to be joined more than once a Moon.

Foon blushed a little at that last thought.

Maybe it wasn't *epic*, exactly.

It was just his first kill. And, sadly, there were no souvenirs or mementos for him to take.

He scolded himself for his moment of pridefulness and straightened up, ready to continue his journey.

The path before him was now completely clear: Up ahead there was a great stairway to descend. Not, probably, to the basement—not yet. There were other perils to face first.

But with a lighter heart after his first triumph, Foon skipped down the hall, feeling far more sure of himself.

TWENTY-FIVE
Night

Clark woke for no reason, eyes wide and staring at the ceiling.

His fear was tempered by confusion: What *was* that all over the ceiling? Little sprinkles of light? Blurry and hard to make out?

Then he remembered the glow-in-the-dark stars.

Then he remembered his Stuffies.

He immediately sat up.

Snowy was there at the end of his bed, but Foon was gone.

Clark started to crawl his way to the end of the bed to see if he had fallen over—then stopped. His pulling of the covers had begun to dislodge and tip Snowy.

He was torn about what to do. If he knocked his last remaining Stuffy onto the floor... Well, he didn't think he had the courage right then to mount a rescue. And then he would be entirely unprotected in bed.

And did he really want to see if Foon was down there on the floor?

Or wasn't?

TWENTY-SIX

Foon's Journey Part III

The steps of the mighty staircase were so high that Foon had to turn onto his stomach and slide down each little cliff. It wasn't dignified, but it worked.

Halfway down he spotted movement at the base of one of the wooden balusters.

Dust Pugs!

Smaller than full-grown Bunnies, bigger than Babies. They chased one another in slow, silly games. Their fuzzy gray bodies made them almost invisible in the gloom.

"Well met," Foon called out formally. It was the right thing to do, despite the ridiculousness of the creatures.

"A Stuffy!" one cried out. It stopped its game, and the others bounced around it and on top of it, trying to get a better view.

"We haven't seen any of your kind in *ages*," said one. "At least *two days!*"

"Where is your fur?" said another.

"Why are you leaving your Boy's Room?" asked the largest one, one who knew a little more about the House and how it worked.

"I'm rescuing my comrades held captive in the basement," Foon said gravely.

Several of the Dust Pugs shuddered, but others did not. They had kin even in those evil places. Basement Bunnies were less furry, more inclined to sharp edges and metal thorns.

"I am new to this House and could use any help or information you might give me."

"Don't go into the basement alone," the largest one said. It was hard to tell if the thing was being flip or serious.

"Outer walls often have windows, up and far away," another put in.

"The best food comes from under the mats," said a third.

"Beware the Monster that guards the crossing," said the tiniest one of all.

Foon blinked in surprise.

He bent down low to look closely at the fuzzy ball before him. She seemed to shimmer, and bounced less randomly than her brethren.

"Where is this Monster? What crossing?"

"She means the door to the basement," the largest one said. "It guards the door...."

But then the Pug rolled and rolled right off the step. A half-dozen of the smaller ones were pulled along in the bits of hair and fun. Their soft giggles didn't echo at all in the darkness as they disappeared.

Very quickly Foon found himself alone.

He decided he had to be content with this news; indeed, it was amazing that he got anything at all from the shiftless and undependable Dust Bunnies.

He threw himself onto his belly and continued to slide down the rest of the stairs.

FOON

i no what youre thinking. why Foon talk so big and special in story FOONS JOURNEY but not in parts called FOON. is reason. u will find out.

TWENTY-SEVEN
Foon's Journey Part IV

The stairs ended just before the Front Door, beyond which lay madness and insanity and the wide open yonder. Foon felt lucky to have been there—carried safely in a bag between the car and the House. Maybe someday he would be able to brave it without a Calling, like from the bear or the Moon. But not yet.

To the east lay the living room: a giant realm of darkness, sofas, and chairs, that was neither welcoming nor threatening. Without any humans it certainly wasn't comfortable, but there was no immediate danger. Monsters almost never prowled these rooms, especially ones that were used often and had TVs.

To the west was a dim light. Perhaps, even if it was the wrong way, Foon could gain his bearings there. He strode toward it, spear at the ready.

As soon as he crossed the threshold his soft feet slid on the slippery linoleum. Foon had found the kitchen. And where there was a kitchen, there might be help.

He tipped his head back to take in the sky-scraping counters, the massive white mountain of the fridge. There were provisions available for those who required them: fresh water and tidbits and nibbles under the stove. Foon was above such mundane needs. He continued to pad silently across the floor, looking for something else.

"GREETINGS, TINY STUFFY," boomed a mechanical voice from above.

Foon tried not to wince, his presence now thoroughly announced to all. But of course there were no Monsters here: where there were friendly Ap-Lionses, there never would be. As the other Stuffies had told him, they were a proud race, fierce and protective of their Family, often kind and sometimes even jovial.

Foon looked around until he found the source of the voice. It was something tall and clear as crystal, partially obscured from his view because of its position on the back of the counter.

"Good evening, kind sir or madam," Foon said with a modest bow. He remembered the formal words and phrases the blue Stuffy had taught him, that these people liked and used. "May the Electricity ever fill you up."

"And may you never get singed as a result. I am the Blender," the Lions said with a smile in its voice. "Are you on a quest to rid this House of the evil that befouls it?"

"Yes," Foon answered, standing tall. "I go first to the basement to rescue my captured comrades. Then together we shall ascend to the highest floor and defeat the King Derker who lurks within the Room of the Parents."

"The highest floor is the attic, but I take your point," the Blender corrected kindly.

"It is good you are going to get help," another voice put in. This was a very shiny—very obviously much loved and protected—Lions, who flipped a lever up and down as it spoke. "I hardly think you could defeat such a beast on your own, so newly made. No offense, little one."

"Would you tell me the way to the basement?"

"It is to the south, over there," the Blender said, whirring its blades. "Around the escarpment on the western side. The door will be on your left."

"I thank you. And I have heard it said a Monster guards the threshold?"

The other Ap-Lions sucked in its metal breath. "Ahh! So that's where the Lomer went. I had wondered, once we chased it away."

"I beg your pardon, fair Lions—"

"I am the *Toaster*, little Stuffy."

"Your pardon, esteemed Toaster, but what is a Lomer?"

"It is what I believe you would call one of the Higher Monsters. Tricky, with some intelligence. They can talk and have individual personalities and terrible hobbies. They are each armed with a single dangerous claw and vicious beak."

An even *Higher* Monster? Were the Silver Fish not enough for him to test his mettle on that night? How many of the greater

Darknesses did this House suffer? He thought he would perhaps have to dispatch a few Feks along the way, maybe some lesser Tahks in the basement...But this?

Foon swallowed, calming himself. Bear thought he was up to the task. He *was* up to the task. He would triumph against the Monster and go down the stairs and rescue his compatriots. And then they would all go after the King Derker together. Just like he planned.

"My dear boy, I don't think your weapon is mighty enough for the Higher Monsters," the Blender ventured.

"It is the spear I was made with," Foon said, a little defensively.

"Yes, and it's lovely...." This was a new voice, a kindly one, from a Lions he couldn't see at all. "But he's right, dear. You've already drawn first blood, and it's time you had something more suitable for a knight of your stature. I speak as the Espresso Machine. And I know just the thing. In the drawer, there."

Foon backed up as a drawer slowly opened itself high above his head. Far out of reach. Its hidden contents glittered against the ceiling.

Had he known these Lionses better and lived in this House longer, he might have presumed to ask one to lower its cord so that he could climb up it. To do so now, however, would be incredibly rude.

Foon frowned at the drawer, gauging its height.

Then he began to run.

Straight at the cabinet.

At the last minute he thrust his spear down, practically burying its tip in the linoleum. Gripping it tightly and using all his strength, he vaulted up and over its top, flying higher than he ever could have on his own.

At the pinnacle of his arc he let go of the spear. He tumbled, flailing, grabbing desperately for the handle of the cabinet. His claws struck, and he wrapped them tightly around the slippery metal.

The little Stuffy swung back and forth, kicking his feet helplessly.

"Oh dear," said one of the Lionses.

Foon let himself go slack and just hung there, still.

Then with one mighty kick of both legs at the same time he managed to set his hind claws firmly against the wood panel. Steadily braced, he then pushed and flipped himself over his head and onto the handle. He swayed there, balancing precariously, waving his arms in the air.

The Espresso Maker gasped.

But before gravity could pull him back, Foon quickly scurried the rest of the way up to the counter.

"Bravo!" the Blender shouted enthusiastically.

"Well done!" called the Espresso Machine. He now saw her, all sleek and black and shiny. "Are you all right, dear?" she asked.

"Absolutely, my lady," Foon said, giving her a bow.

"Go and claim your reward, Stuffy! You certainly deserve it. One of the sterling escargot forks should do nicely."

"A mighty trident! For victory!" cried the Toaster.

"A true weapon, befitting a true knight," the Blender said.

Foon peered into the drawer. It was neatly divided into different slots for all sorts of useful weapons, but immediately he saw the one they meant. Off to the side, kept safe with other legendary items like silver ladles and an evil-looking corkscrew, was a shining silver trident.

Foon lifted it up above his head triumphantly. It fit in his paw perfectly and was so well balanced that it barely tipped at all.

"Magnificent!" the Toaster said.

"A blessing on your quest," the Blender said.

"Better move it along, then," the Espresso Machine suggested. "Time is passing, and morning comes."

Foon gave them all a very low bow.

"Thank you for your gift and your boon. I shall now free my friends and destroy our common enemy."

Then he ran toward the edge of the counter and jumped....

Falling past the cabinet handles, beyond lengths and lengths of wood....

Finally landing in a soft heap on the floor.

He immediately leaped up, saluted those on the counter with his trident, and made for the basement.

"Good-bye!" the Toaster called.

"Pity we can't wake the Vac," the Espresso Maker said after he had gone.

"Yes. He would have made short work of the King Derker, if we could have gotten him upstairs," the Blender agreed with a sigh.

TWENTY-EIGHT
Foon's Journey Part V

The door to the basement was literally just around the corner from the kitchen. As soon as Foon made the turn, the glow from the Lionses' buttons disappeared. Blackness filled the space between that door and the Back Door as if it had oozed in from the larger night beyond.

Foon brandished his new weapon and thought brave thoughts.

Before him was no Monster but a puzzle: The basement door was shut tight. It would be very hard for a little Stuffy to open. With any luck it wasn't locked as well; the Boy and his Sister were old enough for their Parents to be less careful with such things. But it would still take the strength of several Stuffies just to turn the doorknob ... or some very clever tinkering by just one. . . .

As Foon studied the knob, pondering what to do, he realized

that something didn't seem quite right about it. Even in the gloom he could just make out a *darker* thing perched there. It twitched, different depths of oily blacknesses merging and pooling and mixing abominably.

As Foon's button eyes struggled in the low light, the shadow suddenly congealed into one mass. It turned and looked at him, resolving itself into a recognizable shape.

A *sort of* recognizable shape.

It was vaguely like a bird: oval body, short neck, head with a long beak—all of which were the same shade of infinite black. A single leg ended in a single long claw that wrapped around the curve of the golden knob, keeping the thing upright in a very unlikely and precarious manner.

The Monster turned its head this way and that to get a better look at the Stuffy.

Suddenly it stuck its long neck out to examine him, which put its beak into pale rays of the kitchen nightlight.

Foon gasped in horror.

The head, neck, and beak were one smooth, connected object with no borders, no feathers to differentiate them. *And it had no eyes.*

But it was looking at Foon.

"one stuffy they send one but one should go back little stuffy"

"on the other claw stay," it added, shifting on its one and only claw. "button eyes will do but i will need two."

"Come down here and try to take them," Foon cried back.

The creature turned its head to "look" at him from a different position. "little horns tiny fangs eyes seem good, but if not i will grow my collection...."

The Monster twisted and bobbed awkwardly, like it wasn't meant to move, like it wasn't meant to *be*. It didn't seem to have any wings. Suddenly there was a hail of small things that fell tinking onto the floor. Foon stood his ground bravely, holding up his trident to protect his face, thinking it was an attack.

Then he saw what they were.

Eyes.

Button eyes.

And some that weren't even buttons: Some were actual eyes, round and blue glass with big black centers, orange plastic with slits like a cat's, solid black and tiny, like on all the cute little Stuffies who came from drugstores. There must have been a dozen of those.

Foon staggered back, feeling sick.

The thing on the doorknob threw its head back in what appeared to be laughter, but no sound came out.

"tinkle tinkle nice collection tinkerfalls, but i try them on sometimes."

It turned its head away for a moment and when it looked back at Foon, it was no longer blind: On one side of its head a single googly eye was stuck, all cartoonish and goofy. On the other side of its head was a doll's eye, soft brown and complete with eyelashes.

Foon tried not to look away, but it was hard. Before him was the most horrible thing he had ever seen in his short life—worse than the most horrible thing he could *imagine*. What had happened to the Stuffies and Dolls whose eyes it had taken? Were they still in the House? Were they the ones held captive in the basement?

Or was this collection from more than one House? How old was this thing? Did it go from one Family to the next, taking the eyes here and there and then moving on?

"now i need bigger eyes better eyes better for seeing," the Monster said thoughtfully. It winked and the two eyes it wore fell off, also to the floor, shed as easily as a loose tail feather.

Foon leaped out of the way in disgust.

He scolded himself: A true warrior never reacted on feelings alone.

The thing was *trying* to rattle him. That was obvious.

He should save his strength for the battle against the King Derker, later, in the Parents' Room.

But he couldn't stop thinking about Stuffies missing eyes.

White-hot rage, new to the little Stuffy, consumed him.

How dare this Monster be allowed to *be*. How dare it touch Stuffies with its evil claw and desecrate their faces by stealing their eyes!

Without thinking Foon reached back and flung his trident as hard as he could.

The Monster squawked, almost like a real bird, caught off guard by the Stuffy's sudden and violent attack.

But the trident didn't connect with its body, as Foon had

intended. It buried itself in the one leg instead. The Monster tumbled, dragging the weapon behind. It made a terrible *clank* as it hit the metal doorknob.

The Lomer lifted up into the air on stumpy masses that flowed from him and were almost like wings. But also not at all like wings.

Foon cursed his aim.

The Lomer flapped awkwardly and clumsily, trying to escape into the living room, through the doorway opposite the kitchen. A rain of eyes dribbled out of its body.

Foon ran after it, leaping and trying to grab his weapon back. But he was too short.

He looked around for something else to hurl at the Monster. The only things around him were the eyes, and he shuddered at the thought of using them.

What could he do?

Then it came to him: Maybe if he couldn't get his trident back, he could at least chase the Lomer toward the kitchen, where the Lionses could take care of it.

He ran, putting himself between the path to the living room and the Monster. He leaped and waved his paws and made himself as big and threatening-looking as possible. He hissed and threw his mouth open, exposing the full length of his tusks. He snapped his head back, showing off the points of his horns.

The Monster beat its awful wings twice as fast to avoid the dangerous little Stuffy, nearly colliding with him. It flapped and scrabbled desperately, trying to climb into the air again, dragging the spear and the tip of its single greasy claw against the floor.

Foon threw himself at the dangling leg. He slid off it like it was liquid, nothing to grasp.

The Monster took off toward the kitchen, bouncing between the walls as it went.

The trident came tumbling out of its flesh. It fell to the floor with a much healthier sound than the eyes made.

"Our old enemy is back!" came a mechanical voice from the kitchen.

"It is wounded! Let us finish the job the Stuffy began!"

"To arms!"

Foon heard the sounds of whirring blades starting up.

He sighed in relief. While he didn't defeat the enemy himself, at least his plan had worked. The point was to defeat the Monsters, not to pursue glory. The Lomer was doomed.

Foon picked up his trident delicately in his paws: Two of the three tines were bent—and not even in the same direction.

He didn't allow himself to grieve at the damage. The mangled points were a good lesson and reminder for the future. He would never again let an enemy manipulate him into rage. From now on he would always remain firm and focused when battling a Monster.

"Thank you for teaching me this," Foon told his weapon, holding it up above his head. "I name you—*Focus.*"

He cleaned the tines as best he could, wiping away the smeary black Monster offal.

Then he looked around the battlefield. Dozens of eyes lay discarded and strewn about the floor.

Foon would not abandon them to be swept up by a well-meaning but myopic Parent, or vacuumed up reluctantly. But he had no satchel or any proper bag.

He considered the problem for a few moments. Then he took the longest unbent tine on his weapon and carefully picked open a single stitch on his body seam, making a small hole.

Looking hard to make sure he didn't miss any, he gathered all the eyes and stuffed them, one by one, into his own body.

When they were all safely tucked away he tied a knot over the hole as best he could with his soft, large paws. Moving was a little strange now, the eyes flowing around his body and filling in the empty spaces with little clicks. He wondered if this was what it was like to be a beanbag. Then he returned to the puzzle of how to get into the basement.

But the doorknob had been turned—and the door was open a crack.

Maybe it happened when the Monster was trying to get away. Maybe it was fate rewarding him for his trials thus far. Maybe it was just luck. Whatever the reason, the path was wide and the way clear.

Foon began his journey downward.

TWENTY-NINE
Night

Clark didn't think he would actually fall asleep again, but suddenly he was sitting up in bed, heart racing. Awake, when he hadn't been the moment before.

There were ... *sounds* coming from downstairs.

Tiny, faraway sounds.

Like mice were in the kitchen, or jumping about in the mud room—his mom's fancy name for the mats and hooks near the back door.

Except of course the Smiths never had mice.

Okay, *once.* His mom went on a rampage and set traps and found the nest ... and then the otherwise heartless killer of mice personally nursed the orphaned babies until they were grown up and let them go in the woods a few miles away.

But Clark had been very young then, and Mrs. Smith had

done everything in her power to prevent that sort of thing from ever happening again. So, not mice.

So if not mice, then...what?

Clark scrunched down in his bed, putting his pillow over his head.

"Good luck, Foon," he whispered.

THIRTY

Foon's Journey Part VI

The yawing abyss of the basement lay below him. He could feel rather than see the vast, empty space that unfolded beyond the stairs: a cavern so wide and deep that it made its own weather. The air was moist and dank and smelled *off* to his yarn nose. Little wisps of subterranean breezes chased each other unnaturally above the floor.

Foon surveyed the stairs cautiously. He didn't want to expose his back to anything hiding below, so slipping backward on his belly was out of the question.

Shuffling to the edge of the first step, he peered down, judging its height. Not *too* bad. He leaned all the way over, planted his trident on the step below—and slid down around it like it was a pole.

He did it again, to the next step. *Thunk, twirl,* land.

Thunk, twirl, land.

Hopefully he was doing it quietly enough that no one would be alerted to his presence. Hopefully he would get to the bottom undetected, thereby gaining the advantage of surprise—

WOOMP.

Bright lights snapped on, blinding him.

Foon staggered, throwing his paws up to shield his eyes from the glare. Sparks of pain exploded in his Stuffy head.

What sort of Monster was this? Most *hid* from light; they were creatures of the Dark.

Maybe it was some obscure creature that Foon hadn't learned about yet. Maybe it was something undead and hideous with lanterns for eyes. Maybe it was a Lions gone rogue.

Foon waved his weapon sightlessly before him, hoping to scare away any attackers while he recovered.

As soon as the pain relented a little he forced his eyes open. Halos of stinging fire still danced before him. But what he finally saw there...

Made him laugh at himself.

Boring, harmless, plastic, white rectangular lights. There to illuminate the stairwell for the Family. Like a very cleverly arranged trap, the lights had come on when Foon stepped in front of them. They were almost like Lionses, and certainly not of the Dark.

But it was still unfortunate. Now everything in the basement knew that *something* was coming.

On the other paw, perhaps the lights would scare Dark-loving Monsters away. Luck was sometimes like that.

Foon took a deep breath and continued on his way down, horns alert for the slightest noise.

As soon as his hind feet touched the stone floor he braced himself. Ready for the attacks to begin. Basements were prime Monster territory. They often had more than one portal to the Darkness, according to his friends from the Circle of Fire. Sometimes there were whole fleets of Tahks skittering on their bony claw tips across cold, stony floors. Slokah coiled in the corners where it was dampest. Ghellish hung like slime from the ceiling, their thin, wet membranes clinging to whatever surface stuck out and gave them a good hold.

Foon scanned every square inch he could see—easier now, with the light—and listened.

Nothing.

He squinted at the ceiling, but there were no Ghellish. There *might* have been a Cowber or two in the corners, just outside the range of the light, but they were silent and skittish.

Foon quickly looked back down, left and right, in case anything was sneaking by while he looked elsewhere.

Nothing.

That was odd.

Even the safest basements had a *couple* of the lesser Monsters.

Suspicious, he walked forward slowly. With a King Derker, Silver Fish, and a Lomer *up*stairs, it didn't seem likely that this place was entirely empty of evil.

So what had driven them away?

"where . . . ere. We."

Foon spun, looking around wildly. He could have sworn he heard a faint, high-pitched voice.

He waited, hoping to hear it again. He turned his head this way and that, using his horns like giant radio antennas to pick up signals.

". . . sds! Vrem! Mmm!"

There!

He ran forward, holding his trident at the ready.

Humongous machinery of unfathomable purpose rose to the right and left of him. Strange clicks and hisses that sounded like Monsters actually came from giant metal boxes and tanks. An ugly tangle of pipes snarled around themselves before exploding out into every direction. Some were cold and slick, dripping their icy sweat onto the floor. Some were dry and hot like a fevered brow.

Foon tried not to be distracted by all this. He kept his eyes ahead, looking for the source of the voice.

Was that it? At the end of this endless Room was—perhaps— the goal of his quest. Next to an ancient set of shelves piled with rusty bits and things sat an enormous, perfectly clean garbage bag. It was stuffed to its limit, the top tied in a neat bow.

There was definitely movement under the filmy surface of the bag.

Foon drew back, horrified by the strange impressions the shapes made, stretching and distending the plastic. It seemed Monstrous.

Then the shapes shifted excitedly and he heard more sounds from inside.

"Mmmm! Mmsssssff!"

Tiny voices.

Stuffy voices.

Stuffies!

What?!?

This was what happened to his compatriots? The friends he hadn't met yet? They were crammed into a garbage bag—like garbage? To be thrown *out*?

Foon was outraged. That bow at the top—that wasn't the work of any Monster. That was a Big Person, a Parent.

Stuffies. Treated like garbage.

It was…unheard of.

"Fellow Stuffies," Foon called out, after he had recovered himself. "I am here to rescue you. After I set you free we must hurry back before the light of dawn and dispatch the King Derker who lurks upstairs. Stand aside, so I may cut a hole without injuring you."

The high voices grew louder, squeakier, and more strident. Still he couldn't make out what they were saying.

"Hold a moment," he said. Aiming carefully, he used the tip of his trident to poke a very small hole in the bag. Then, a little awkwardly because of his blunt paws, he reached in and stretched out the hole as best he could.

The hoof of an old horse immediately popped out. This Stuffy was definitely loved: His pelt was majestic and worn, regal and ancient. Foon would have bowed or offered some other sign of respect, but the other Stuffy interrupted him before he had a chance.

"No! It's a trap!" the horse cried. "The Monster is *here....*"

And then the automatic lights went out.

THIRTY-ONE
Foon's Journey Part VII

Foon dropped into ready stance, gripping his trident tightly.

The voices in the garbage bag went silent.

Everything was still.

And then—a low, throaty laugh came from *behind* the bag.

With a slow, oily uncoiling, the King Derker revealed itself.

The Monster was just like Foon had imagined. And worse.

It had a giant head like a sick distortion of a dragon's, the angles and features all wrong. Its lower jaw was too big and dragged on the floor, scraping the dust with its beard. Scales that were also too big overlapped one another poorly, growing more and more jagged on the top of its head until they formed a fleshy crown—the distinguishing characteristic of a King Derker. Its eyes were so tiny and black they were almost lost in its face.

And this was at the end of a body that was far too skinny to even support such a head. Tail, neck, and torso were all the same thin width. Hundreds of appendages that were either floppy legs or short tentacles were unevenly spaced along its wretched length.

"Well, well. Look at *you*," the Monster said, continuing to coil around the garbage bag with the rest of its body while keeping its head and face steady, eyes fixed on Foon. "*You're* the one they've sent to rescue these prisoners? You're all they have left? I think I'm insulted. You're nothing but a...mishmash, a ragtag, an unfit bundle of cloth. Useless."

The Derker was just taunting him, throwing out insults that didn't even make sense. Foon's strength lay in the very fact he was made by hand, whatever his material was. But the smarter Monsters could be tricky. He had to be careful not to be hypnotized by its words or movements.

"And yet I am here, to rescue my comrades," he said, raising his trident.

"Ohhh... I see it now," the Monster said, mock pensively. "You thought you would come down here and free your little friends...then all of you would return to the upstairs to defeat me, as one big happy army.

"Surprise!"

The King Derker thrust its head forward. Foon jumped back.

The Monster laughed.

"Ah, Stuffies. Always so predictable. Of course that was your plan. Of course I came down here to wait for you. There always seems to be a..., *you*. Left under a radiator, found behind a shelf, under a pile of clothes...Stragglers. You are not the first, trust me, little Stuffy."

It licked its lips.

Foon tried not to shudder.

"Impressive, isn't it?" It turned to look at the garbage bag. Its body began to coil in the opposite direction, making Foon dizzy. "I'm very proud of my little mountain of captured Stuffies. It took some doing, let me tell you.

"At first it seemed easy. I drained the Father of his will— and delicious it was, too! How rare it is that one of us gets to feed on an Adult. Their juice is...richer...more complex... full-bodied. Perhaps I grew too sure of myself. Too cocky, fed, *stuffed*, if you will, on his essence.

"So I went after the Mother. She was— She was completely without weakness. Impenetrable. Strong. I could make no inroads with that one."

Foon felt a stirring of pride for the Boy's Mother. True, she hadn't said the kindest things about him when he was first made, but she was obviously a warrior.

"As it turned out, I didn't need to consume her. She already had ideas of her own...about growing up, about cleaning, and about...*getting rid of ssstttuff.*"

The monster hissed, rising several feet into the air above the garbage bag, tentacles waving. Mismatched metallic teeth scraped against each other in a hideous grin. Foon winced at the high-pitched noises they made.

"All I needed to do then was give her a nudge—through the

Father, of course. He was easy to sssway. 'Time for the Boy to move on.' 'Maybe get rid of a few things.' 'He needs to start acting more like a Man.'"

Foon's horns curled in horror: The Monster had changed its voice so it sounded *exactly* like the Father. It was like it was already halfway to becoming him.

"Oh, I do love whispering my ideas into the minds of others." It slowly lowered itself back down to Foon's level and regarded him closely. "She gathered up the lot and tossed them away. All in the name of growing up."

The whole time the Monster had been talking, Foon was thinking furiously. Planning, trying to figure out what to do. Though this Monster was far smarter than the other things that haunted the House, the Derker wasn't *quite* as clever as it thought. Also it had a tendency to boast. Maybe there was an advantage to be had in this.

"But how did you—a *King*—come to haunt this House and Family?" Foon asked, trying to make it sound like he cared. "I have never heard of such a thing. Monsters don't feed off Grownedups."

"Oh, it happens from time to time," the Monster said modestly. It swayed thoughtfully, cocking its head as if recalling other instances.

Foon crept just the tiniest bit closer to the bag.

"I am certainly not the *first* to accomplish such a thing," it continued. "Though such grand achievements are few and far between."

Foon moved a little nearer.

The old horse, who was stuck halfway out of the bag, turned its head as if to question what he was doing. Foon shook his own head very slightly. *Keep still!*

"This Father has brought with him a...history," the Monster went on. "A history that caught up with him thanks to a box of old forgotten toys and memories, sent by his parents. Jack-in-the-box, crank the handle, and out pops—ME!"

Ever so slowly, Foon reached out his paw toward the hole in the bag. He kept his eyes on the Monster, trying to look genuinely interested.

"And here he is, still ripe to receive old, Dark ideas. Now we have invaded his very body and mind. He is almost entirely ours. Soon. It will not be long. I will be wearing the hands and feet of a Person and bring Darkness to the rest of the world...NO!"

The Derker's head snapped close to Foon, a hairbreadth from his face. The Stuffy froze, his paw just touching the plastic bag, prepared to rip the hole wide open.

"No," the Monster said with a grin. "You shall not get any help from your friends. I will devour you, brave little knight, and leave your innards as a warning to anyone else who should come.

"Soon I will lay my eggs in the small monkey, its Stuffing so soft and perfect. And my kith shall grow, and the Darkness shall own this House and make it ours. And from here we will go forth and spread our filth and disease across the world!"

Foon tried to think of something to say. Heroic, brave, defiant...but nothing came to his little stuffed head.

So he took his trident and jabbed it into the face of the Monster.

It threw its ugly head back, screaming. Its body lashed around on the floor. The trident stayed stuck in its flesh.

And then Foon ran.

THIRTY-TWO
Foon's Journey Part VIII

He dashed around to the back of the garbage bag, raking his paws along it. No good. Although they could do mighty damage to Monsters, on objects in the real world his claws were no sharper than soft cloth. At best he stretched and thinned out the plastic a little.

"Brothers and Sisters!" he cried. "Struggle, do your best to get out! I do not believe I can fight this thing alone!"

"We shall do our best!" the horse called back to him. "As one, comrades! *PUSH!*"

There was a mighty roar from the Monster. Foon heard a *tink* as his trident was yanked from the thing's flesh and skittered across the stony floor.

When he came around to the front side of the bag again, the Derker was shaking itself, recovering from the blow. Black ichor dotted the ground and pooled around a giant torn scale.

Foon put his head down and charged, slamming his horns into the monster's back.

The Derker let out another howl. It whipped its tail at Foon, striking hard and sending the Stuffy flying.

He tumbled through the cold air of the basement, horns over heels, hitting the ground with a soft *splat*. Immediately he leaped up and patted himself down, shaking his legs and arms to get the Stuffing back where it needed to be. The dozens of little plastic eyes inside him actually made it a bit easier to fix his center of gravity.

The Derker was fully raging now, roaring and pacing madly in front of the bag.

Foon wasted no time. He ran forward, again keeping his head low.

The Monster also lowered its head, preparing for another charge.

At the last moment Foon fell away to the right. He grabbed the sharp, ugly Derker scale on the ground without stopping and continued to run toward the bag.

He dragged the scale's sharpest end along the plastic. Like everything about the Monster itself, it wasn't perfect, and it didn't cut the neat line Foon had hoped. But it did catch the plastic here and there and rip little bits out.

Immediately the Stuffies inside begin to push and work their way against the slits. Arms, legs, tails, and heads stuck through the holes, trying to make them bigger.

The Derker screamed. It bunched itself up like a caterpillar and sprang at Foon, its mouth wide and gaping.

Foon kept running, zigging and zagging away from the bag, making himself a more difficult target.

It didn't work.

Too soon he felt the hot, fetid breath from the Derker's mouth right before it snapped shut. Foon threw himself to the side—

But he wasn't fast enough.

A dozen razor-sharp teeth closed on the cloth of his shoulder, slicing it to shreds.

The little Stuffy fell to the ground. His right arm dangled uselessly, and the giant hole where his shoulder had been now leaked Stuffing. Several plastic eyes fell out, tinkling on the ground.

Foon grasped the wound with his left paw. The pain was incredible. But he was a warrior and would not heed it. All wounds could be fixed later. What was important was destroying the Monster *now*.

Which...he was not going to be able to do if he was still alone. He was no match for such a beast.

The Derker still had a bit of sock from Foon's shoulder left in its teeth and was shaking it back and forth triumphantly. While the Monster was distracted doing this, Foon risked a look at how the Stuffies were doing. The old horse was halfway out, pawing the air with his hooves and desperately throwing himself left and right, trying to squeeze his haunches through. More talons and claws and feet were out and ripping the holes, but no one was free yet.

And, Foon realized, he had dropped the Derker's scale at some point. Probably when his arm was ripped off.

He needed a weapon—he had to find his trident. It was the only way to kill the Monster and free his friends. But where had it fallen? He had blurry images of it sliding into the far corner of the basement, the one toward the steps that led Outside. He ran, his wound shedding Stuffing as he went.

The Monster growled and slithered after him.

Foon took a random path, circling around potential obstacles when he could. Sometimes he stopped suddenly and let the Monster shoot out past him—before turning and running the opposite way.

But he could never shake the thing for very long. Its hideous panting and the foul breath on his neck were a constant reminder of its imminent attack.

Finally Foon spotted a dull gleam in a pile of dust completely empty of Dust Bunnies. His trident! He threw himself toward it, sliding across the floor on his knees.

The Monster saw what he was doing.

It whipped the end of its tail like a scorpion over both its and Foon's heads. The barbed end caught the tip of the trident, flinging it away. The weapon spun across the floor, wedging itself under the garbage bag.

Foon cursed—and then rolled quickly to the side as the Monster lunged at him.

He took off again, back toward the bag, not bothering to try outmaneuvering the enemy. His only chance now was to get his weapon back as fast as possible.

The Derker must have realized what Foon intended to do. It launched its sinuous body through the air like the tail of a kite and managed to land in front of him. There was no way the Stuffy could stop himself from colliding with it.

So Foon opened his mouth as wide as it would go. As he smashed into the wall of Monster flesh he chomped down—hard.

The Derker shrieked, throwing itself up and backward. Foon kept his tusks locked even as the horrible thing spun and lashed and threw itself around, trying to get the Stuffy off.

It slammed its body against the ground, Foon along with it. Stuffing got wadded up badly in the back of his head. The pain was almost unbearable.

They looped and wormed and dove around the basement, Foon hanging on by his teeth. The Monster roared like a steam train. It brushed against an overhanging pipe trying to scrape the little Stuffy off.

Instead, Foon grabbed onto the pipe with both his front and hind paws and clung desperately.

The King Derker was yanked to a stop. Foon's tusks were buried too deeply into its flesh for it to snap free.

It hung, stunned, from Foon's mouth, many of its hind tentacles drifting against the floor.

Foon let go of the pipe, and they fell together, hard, onto the cold cement below. The Derker tried to raise itself up on its fore-tentacles, shaking its head in confusion. Foon grabbed the closest thing he saw—a piece of wood from a pile of kindling—and slammed it over its head.

Again, and again, and again.

Finally it lay still.

Its eyes unfocused and grew cloudy.

Foon kept the piece of wood raised . . . but the Derker didn't stir.

It was over.

The little Stuffy finally dropped the stick and shuddered in exhaustion. He had lost a lot of Stuffing, and the Room was beginning to swim in front of his eyes.

He could barely see the old horse finally emerge from the hole in the giant black bag, tumbling softly onto the floor.

"Good show, well done!" he neighed, spotting Foon and waving excitedly. Foon waved wearily back. "A King Derker! And you defeated him on your *own!* They'll be singing about this for ages! Now let's get the others free!"

Foon gave him a paws-up, too winded to respond. He tried to remember where his trident was since it would make much quicker work of the bag with its sharp points. Ah, there—under the other side of the bag now rapidly emptying of Stuffies. He slowly made for it, stumbling a little as he went. He had to lean on the bag for support when he bent to pick it up.

Suddenly the horse screamed. *"WATCH OUT!"*

The Derker slammed its horned head into Foon's back, barreling him into a wall.

When it pulled away, the little Stuffy slid down to the floor. He did not get up immediately this time.

The Monster took a moment to examine its wounds. It growled in fury at a pair of giant black, oozing holes where Foon's tusks had been.

Then it howled and dove at the Stuffy.

Foon forced himself up. He *made* his short legs move, faster than they ever had before. But the whole right side of his body wasn't working properly. Most of the stitches there had popped while the Monster was trying to shake him off. His run was lopsided, and he kept listing in a circle.

"Your weapon!" the horse shouted.

He grabbed the trident and tossed it to Foon.

The Monster charged, all speed and teeth and scales.

"For the Velveteen," Foon whispered, summoning his last bit of strength.

He leaped up toward his trident, which arced sparklingly through the air.

He tumbled awkwardly the last few inches—but his left paw closed around the weapon. Foon grinned, feeling the hard, friendly heft of the shaft.

He turned, aiming it at the heart of the Monster.

"The Darkness shall *never win!*"

And then the Monster got him.

FOON

no no dougnut be upset!!!!
im fine. keep reeding!

THIRTY-THREE

Day

Clark opened his eyes and quietly regarded the new starry ceiling.

He had made it through the night.

Sunlight sparkled across his room in a way he didn't remember it doing before. Had the rays always reached that far in? Had they always been so wide?

He sat up, blinking. The air smelled... sweet. When he breathed in, it was like he got more oxygen than he normally did. His heart began skipping.

For no good reason it felt like the beginning of the best day he ever had.

Snowy was cuddled into his side. Foon was nowhere to be seen, but somehow Clark wasn't worried. He bet that the little Stuffy was somewhere in the house with all the other ones.

He leaped out of bed and pattered down the hall. It wasn't

just his recently redone room that seemed fresh and hopeful. The old squeaky floorboards glowed like antique gold and a fresh breeze played between the paneled walls. He looked into his sister's room. Anna was actually awake—which was miracle enough. She was sitting up in bed, blinking, just the way he had been a few moments before.

"It feels like... Christmas?" she said, scratching the back of her head in confusion.

Yes! That was exactly it. It felt like the day was going to be wonderful. That *every* day could be wonderful.

What a weird sensation.

"What's going on?" she asked him, almost accusingly.

"I don't know!" he answered with a grin.

But he had a hunch.

He practically leaped the distance to his parents' room.

His mother was in the bathroom. He could hear her— singing!—around her toothbrush.

His dad was sitting up on the edge of their bed. He still looked tired, but there was a pinkness in his cheeks Clark hadn't seen in a while. Hedwig the Hippokoukou was still on the bed, between his and Mrs. Smith's pillows. Clark gave the Stuffy a wink.

"Hey," Mr. Smith said slowly, as if coming out of a very deep sleep. "When was... when was the last time we went to a baseball game?"

Clark laughed. "We've *never* been to a baseball game, Dad. Like, a real one."

"Well, I don't like baseball," his father said, thinking about it. "I love soccer, though. We should all go to a soccer game. Or a NASCAR race. I've always wanted to see one of those."

"Or . . . a monster truck rally?" Clark suggested hesitantly.

His dad smiled. "If we have to. If everyone wants to. I feel like your sister put you up to that, though."

Honestly, it was the first fun thing that came into Clark's head. If he had a choice, he would rather have gone to Medieval Times or a Renaissance Faire, but maybe there would be a chance to fix that later.

"As long as we're all hanging out, it doesn't matter," Mr. Smith said with a smile. He reached over and fluffed Clark's hair, then pulled him into a quick hug.

Mrs. Smith came out of the bathroom, face shiny with recent cosmetic scrubbing.

"Hey, buddy! Isn't it a great day?"

Then she looked confused for a moment. She was always saying things like that, motivational phrases like *What's the best thing about right now?* and *You're a rock star!* and *The greatest day ever is today.* But when she said *these* words just now, it was like she realized today it was actually true. She smiled and laughed as if she had said something silly.

Clark laughed, too.

The Monster was gone.

There was no other possible explanation.

The doom on the house was lifted. The air was cleared.

There were no shadows, no smog, *nothing* haunting the corners now. Clark had brought Foon home, and somehow he and the other Stuffies had managed to fix things for good.

He had to thank the little guy. Immediately. He began to look for him: under the bed, throwing open drawers, peeping in the closet where his parents hid his birthday presents.

"Clark, what are you doing?" his mom demanded.

"Have you seen Foon?"

"What? Who— Oh, that doll your grandma made. No, I haven't."

"Did you come into my room at night and—rearrange stuff?" he asked, still going through his mother's bureau.

"No, Clark, I said no, now cut that out," she said, exasperated, closing the drawers behind him.

He ran out of their room, resisting the urge to call out *Foon, Foooo-ooon*. He looked in every room upstairs—even, briefly, Anna's. Nothing. He went downstairs, pausing halfway down to get an aerial view of the living room. Nothing was out of order—except for the icky feel of a dust bunny on his toe. He shook it off and ran down the rest of the way, throwing pillows from the couches and looking under everything that could hide anything.

He even looked in the kitchen, which was as safe and clean and light blue and boring as ever.

He stood in front of the basement door.

Since they had built a laundry room on the main floor there

was no reason for him ever, *ever*, to go down there. Anna sometimes had to when she was dealing with the household trash, but that was it.

Clark frowned. On the floor, in front of the slightly open door, was something small and shiny and round.

He bent over and picked it up.

It was an eye.

Not one of Foon's button eyes. A real doll eye, with a special nubbin for attaching it permanently to cloth. What the heck? Clark didn't have any stuffed animals with eyes like that, and none of Anna's dolls had them, either.

It made him extremely uneasy. He slipped it into his pocket, took a deep breath, and opened the door.

"Hello?" he called. Then he flipped on the light—the automatic ones his mom put in to save energy were never enough to scare away all the shadows.

He descended slowly. On every step he wanted to pause, to turn back, to run away.

But . . . *Foon*. The little guy had obviously dealt with whatever was infecting the house. He owed it to the Stuffy to look for him, even in the darkest, blackest corners. They all did.

And Clark had braved the woods by himself. The basement of his own home was nothing in comparison.

Right?

When he got to the bottom step he held his breath and ran for the next real light, not feeling safe until its cord was firmly in his hand. He pulled, and its ugly, wonderful white light flooded the next fifteen feet.

At the edge of which Clark saw something that immediately outraged him.

A *garbage bag*. Filled with his Stuffies! Like his mom was planning on *throwing them out!*

He ran forward, forgetting his fear. The bag had tipped over and was full of holes. Stuffies were spilling out of it on all sides.

Strange... there was a careful little pile of them that had somehow formed *next* to the bag.

And in the middle of that pile was Foon.

Well, most of him.

Clark suddenly felt sick.

Foon's head had been torn off. His tail dangled by a single thread. One arm and one leg were missing. Both of his eyes looked like they had been chewed. There was stuffing everywhere.

"No," Clark sobbed, collapsing onto the floor.

FOON

*no no, member: im reeding story
with u. <u>not</u> ded. reed, reed!*

THIRTY-FOUR

Still Day

His parents, of course, said the expected parent things.

"A rat must have gotten in down here."

"Geez—it's totally torn apart, like whatever animal got in here thought it was really real."

"Raccoon maybe? I don't see any tracks."

"Things do look a bit scuffed up on the floor... I think. It's hard to tell...."

"We should call the exterminator."

Clark quietly wept over Foon.

He got on his hands and knees and scoured the basement, looking for all of the Stuffy's missing parts and stuffing. He found frayed yarn, clumps of fluff, his arm—and a fancy little fork that *wasn't* Foon's original weapon, but somehow looked like it belonged with him.

He also found several dozen more plastic and glass eyes. Which was very weird.

"Hm" was all Anna said, thoughtfully.

"Geez, I'm sorry, buddy, that's terrible," his dad said, looking perplexed.

"Clark, I . . . I'm really sorry." Mrs. Smith sat down on the floor—right in the dust, in her clean tan pants. She put her arms around him. "I didn't . . . I never thought anything would happen to them down here."

Clark sniffed and let himself be hugged. His mom gently touched the edge of Foon's mouth, where one tusk dangled uselessly. "I don't think I ever *really* understood how much they mean to you."

For once his mom had no idea what to do, nothing to say, no way to make things better. Clark didn't say *It's okay* because it wasn't. He just leaned against her, feeling a little of the calm that comes after crying.

At least she was beginning to understand; that was something.

"Hey," she said slowly, after a moment. "Maybe your grandmother can fix him."

THIRTY-FIVE

Day

Getting to see Grandma Machen was both more and less complicated than Clark expected. He could see her the very next
day... but only at the hospital, where she was having her chemo
done.

"It's good you're coming," Anna said. She was driving, which
was a little weird. Before all this happened she was rarely allowed
to take the car, and never with Clark in the backseat. Their mom
was in the front seat, working, constantly jabbing at her phone.
Sometimes she slipped her foot out of her sneaker and put it up
on the dashboard to make a bigger lap to work on, and that was
also weird. She acted more like a child when she wasn't driving.

"I don't know," Mrs. Smith said aloud suddenly. She put
her phone down long enough to look worriedly at Clark. "It's a
lot to handle. Seeing all—this. The hospital, the chemo... You
going to be okay?"

"Mom, in other countries kids his age are making shirts and riding bikes two hours to get to school or surviving civil war. He can take this," Anna said sharply.

Clark nodded. He had to be brave for both Foon *and* his grandmother. The Stuffy...what was left of him...was in the Camp I Can daypack clutched on his lap, along with some extra stuffing, needles, thread, scissors, and whatever else he could find that might help.

His grandmother's hospital was different from the one he had to go to when he threw up so much. Things here went much more smoothly. There was no waiting around, no filling out forms, no being told curtly they were going the wrong way. There was no smell of sickness and everyone spoke to them in quiet, kindly voices. There were hand sanitizer stations and little bowls of candy everywhere.

On the third floor they were directed to number thirteen, which was a tiny room past a long hall of tiny rooms. The doors were frosted and when Mrs. Smith carefully slid them aside there was Grandma, like a fancy tropical creature in its habitat at a zoo.

She was in a very comfy-looking chair and had comfy—if plain—blankets snuggling her in. She wore a bright azure ski hat even though it was summer and warm in the room. *Law & Order* was on the TV in front of her and next to her was a pole hung with bags and tubes.

"Hey!" she cried when she saw Clark. "Howza little camper? Big kid now, am I right? Kiss any girls while you were there?"

Clark turned cough-syrup red but hugged her—carefully. She was just as soft as she always was.

"Mom, I'm just going to go make sure all your meds are ready to be picked up," Mrs. Smith said, slipping out.

"We brought some bagels and stuff for lunch," Anna said.

"We'll have a picnic! But, Anna, dear, before you settle, would you mind just getting me some coffee out of the machine?"

"Double espresso, four creamers," Anna recited with a nod and scurried out. Clark's overdressed, dramatic sister. *Scurrying.* The hospital had a strange effect on everyone.

"Now, Clark." Grandma patted the chair next to her and spoke in a low, knowing tone. He had the feeling that she had sent Anna out on purpose, so they could be alone. "I hear there was a problem with Foon."

Clark had promised himself he wouldn't, but tears began to flow again. He knew what his mom would say: Your *grandma* has *cancer* and you're worried about a *stuffed animal?* But he couldn't help it. Things were a little mixed up in his head.

He opened his bag and showed her what was left of the Stuffy.

Grandma Machen's eyes widened and she sucked in her breath. "What the heck happened to him?"

"I found him downstairs. He was all torn up." It was hard to replay the scene again in his mind. "Mom had put . . . all of my other stuffed animals . . . in a garbage bag. . . . He was somehow . . . down there. . . ."

Grandma turned Foon around as best as she could with her

left hand, looking at him over the top of her bright red reading glasses and frowning. She pursed her lips, a thousand tiny lines all sewed up together.

"Anything…different now?" she asked, not naming anything. "New? In the house?"

"Yes—it's *all* better," Clark said, swallowing. "How do you… How do you know about these things? Like Mons—"

"Sssh," his grandmother said, putting a finger to her mouth. "Let's just say that all grandmothers are wise. Wise as children. And some are wiser than others; we don't forget.

"But enough of that. Your father is better, too, I take it?"

"Everything is. Except for Foon."

"Hmm," she said speculatively. Then she took a deep breath, a *cleansing* breath, Mrs. Smith would have said. "Of course he can be fixed. Not exactly the same as new. But just as good. Who knows? Maybe even better."

"So…can you?" Clark asked softly.

"Me? Here? Now?" She held up her right hand, pushing the blanket aside. There were tubes running from her wrist to the bags overhead. There were red marks all over her skin. Puncture wounds. From previous times. "Sorry, kid. No can do."

Clark began to cry.

"I'm sorry! I shouldn't have asked. You're…sick.…It's all… Everything…the Monster…"

"Clark A. Smith." Grandma Machen put Foon down next to her and reached for her grandson impatiently. He let himself

be pulled forward by her surprisingly strong left hand. "This...
your Stuffy, whatever happened, *has nothing to do with my cancer*. Do
you understand?"

Clark nodded, not looking up.

"Do you understand?" she said softer but more firmly. He
finally looked up and nodded.

"My cancer is genetic. Or environmental. Or random. Who
knows. They say mustard is carcinogenic, and I do like my hot
dogs." She said the last bit with a sigh. "I'm beating it; I'll be
done in six months. And it has *nothing to do with you*. Or Monsters.
Okay?"

"Okay," Clark said softly.

"And here's what we're going to do." She took her hand off
Clark and fished around in the blankets for Foon. Her gestures
weren't smooth; it was like she was fighting sleep. But she still
managed to grab the Stuffy and hold him out to Clark. "You
are going to come visit me every week while I get my chemo.
You're going to bring Foon, and thread, and a needle. Or two.
Maybe three. I always lose one. And *you* are going to fix Foon,
under my very judgey eye. You got that, buddy?"

Clark nodded again.

"All right then. And I think you can bring in some movies,"
she added, gesturing at the TV. "We can watch one of your
dragon ones. Or maybe a Star Wars. Haven't seen the latest one.
Come here, Clark."

He didn't want to hurt her, or tangle the tubes, or ruin

something somehow. So he leaned over and scooped his arms out as wide as he could and gathered in her and the blankets and Foon. She reached around with her left arm and squeezed.

Somehow she knew to let go of him right before Anna appeared in the doorway, two steaming cups of coffee in her hands.

"Aren't you a little young for such a big coffee?" Grandma Machen asked archly.

"I'm almost seventeen, Grandma."

"Eh, it'll stunt your growth." But she winked at Clark.

"Oh, uh, Dad texted me," Anna said. The words were strange; she looked confused saying them aloud. He never texted. Not even in emergencies. "He's going to come by here later. We'll all take you home together and order takeout."

"Oh. How lovely. Things *have* changed." She gave Clark another wink. "All right. Anna, give me my coffee. Clark, go find my emergency sewing kit in my bag. Please ignore the two lollipops I saved you for later in there. C'mon now, this patient is in worse condition than *I* am."

And Clark found the needles, and Anna rearranged the tiny, scary-looking table, removing the latex gloves and the packages of lancets and gauze. She laid out a napkin and the coffee and made a nice little setting.

And after bagels and a nice cuppa, they all sat down and began work on Foon.

THIRTY-SIX

Day

It was a quiet, gray Saturday. Clark was in the living room reading. Anna was next to him on the couch, going through college brochures. She sported a small Stuffy monster (not Monster) pin on her lapel: His dozens of eyes were the ones they found in the basement. Clark couldn't decide if this was incredibly creepy or not. He was leaning toward *creepy*. But she had given it a friendly little smile, so maybe it was okay.

Mrs. Smith was in the kitchen with a stack of paperwork, but when Clark went to get a glass of milk she was looking longingly at the cover of a thick paperback. Mr. Smith was installing new memory in their main computer —and hopefully a new game, too.

It was very warm and very moist, and no one much felt like going outside.

"CLARRRK, YOUR FRIEND'S HERE!"

Clark leaped up with joy. He and D. A. had made it to the casual-drop-by level of friendship. The other boy was allowed to bike wherever he wanted as long as he brought his phone so his parents could track him. Clark pushed for similar privileges, but so far had been gently denied.

"H'lo Mr. Smith, Mrs. Smith," D. A. said, letting himself in and heading right for Clark's room, not waiting for him to catch up. "WHOA."

Clark had been organizing his new Pokémon cards earlier. There were dozens of neat stacks piled up all over the floor.

"I just started getting into it when Grandma found a whole collection at a tag sale," Clark said proudly.

"Lucky," D. A. said with an easy jealousy. He nodded his chin at the bed. "How's the little guy doing?"

"Foon's still recovering. But he'll be okay." The Stuffy's mouth was badly twisted from where Clark had tied off the stitches too tightly. He probably didn't speak too well yet. Also the stuffing in his head was wadded up strangely, caught up on itself. Grandma Machen had promised to help her grandson undo it and begin the onerous task of resewing his whole head and face again. As soon as she could use both hands and wasn't so tired. "So—wanna play Pokémon?"

"First you have to see what *I* got."

D. A. proudly stuck out his hands.

In them was a giant, fluffy, sparkling unicorn with a pink mane and tail.

Wearing black, heavy-duty battle armor.

"*WHOA*," Clark said, waggling his fingers, desperate to touch. It was so *shiny*. And *perfect*.

"It was my sister's, she got it at a birthday at Build-A-Bear. Didn't want it anymore. And then my mom found this armor online and three-D printed it at the library. And then I painted it, touched it up a little. Isn't it *sick?*"

Clark took the Stuffy and turned it over in his hands. The armor was hinged and made delicious little clacking noises as the plates shifted against each other. There were tiny studs and spikes decorating it all over. D. A. had done a very neat job highlighting the fire symbol emblazoned on the helmet with gold paint.

"I kind of want to, uh, dye the fur, too," he admitted with a cough. "So it's not pink anymore. But without ruining it."

"This is amazing!" Clark made the unicorn jump through the air and put its head down as if to charge. "ARMOR! This changes everything!"

"Right?" the other boy said, pleased. "I just wish I could show Catherine-Lucille. She would LOVE it. Unicorns in battle armor. That's so her."

"I have her number.... Maybe we could FaceTime her or something?"

"You what? You got her number? You player, you!"

D. A. gave Clark a playful punch on the arm that probably hurt more than he intended—Clark still wasn't used to roughhousing that ended in anything besides wedgies.

They dialed her on D. A.'s phone and triumphantly held up the unicorn.

"I'm right in the middle of something, now, so—HOLY BRIMSTONE WHAT IS THAT?" she swore.

It was a little weird seeing Catherine-Lucille in such a normal situation. She was in a family room with lots of other people talking and moving around in the background. Clark wondered what her house smelled like.

"My mom made the armor on a three-D printer," D. A. explained. "Whatcha think?"

"I think it is utterly amazing," she said, her black eyes dead serious. She still had ponytails; they were flipped to her back.

"Oh, and my dad..." Clark began.

"SHUT IT, PRIVATE. This is not a secure line." Catherine-Lucille leaped up from her couch; the screen was a blurry, dizzy kaleidoscope of colors as she bolted out of the room.

"My dad is fine," Clark said as the blocks rearranged themselves back into his friend's face and she nodded. "Foon got... he got hurt pretty bad. My grandma is helping me fix him up."

"Excellent. That's good to hear."

"Hey, Clark," D. A. said excitedly. "Why don't you make him a set of armor, too? As, like, kind of a get-well present?"

"Oh!" It was a great idea. But... "I don't know how to use a three-D printer or anything."

"REALLY, PRIVATE? YOU NEED SOME FANCY-PANTS TECHNO DOOHICKEY TO MAKE ARMOR FOR YOU? YOU CAN'T FIGURE OUT HOW SOME OTHER WAY?" Catherine-Lucille shouted into the phone, holding it up to her lips so he could read them.

D. A. cracked up. Clark smiled, rightfully chastened.

"Okay, okay," he said. "Maybe we could, I don't know, cut up a milk carton or something? We could go through the recycling and find a takeout box or packing Styrofoam."

"Yeah! Or a soda bottle!" the other boy said enthusiastically.

"And spray-paint it! Anything we want—even silver!" Clark added.

"Okay, but *after* we play with Uni."

"And *after* a game of Pokémon. At which I will beat you into the ground."

"Unlikely, sir. I and my pink-maned unicorn will completely kick your butt."

Catherine-Lucille was quiet. Clark saw that she had a funny look on her face. It was sort of a smile, but she also sort of looked sad.

"Geez. Wish I could come over there and show you guys how it's really done," she mumbled reluctantly. "I'd whip both of you. But good."

The boys grew sober, feeling the girl's envy through the phone.

"I wish you could come, too," Clark said. "It would be way more fun if all of us could hang out together."

The three friends were silent.

"Hey..." Catherine-Lucille began poking at her phone, her fingers filling up part of the screen. "You guys live out near Springfield, right?"

"Kind of. It's not far."

"My cousin's having her quinceañera there, at some stupid event-and-party place. Maybe we could meet up? There's a mall nearby. I could get my dad to drive me, maybe."

"That would be great!"

"Yeah! Sweet!"

A fierce, brief grin flashed over the girl's face before disappearing. Then something happened offscreen and she rolled her eyes.

"Okay, I gotta go. We'll talk more tomorrow!"

"See you!" D. A. called into the phone.

"Bye!" Clark shouted.

"I gotta say, your house smells so much better now," D. A. said after she was off. He took a deep breath. "You can really tell. Something—bad—is gone."

"Yeah, I know."

They both were awkwardly quiet. Monsters didn't bear much talking about aloud, even in daylight hours.

"All right, let's do this!" D. A. suddenly shouted, holding up his unicorn.

They got down on the floor and lined up Clark's strongest Stuffies, going through mock battles and putting the armor-wearing unicorn through her paces.

Clark's mom and dad didn't think he noticed them quietly approach and peek around the doorway, but he did.

They were watching him play with Stuffies. . . .

And smiling.

FOON

sew now u know. i not speak so good
becuz of mowf sewing and Stuffing
stuffed rong places in hed. but ill
get better. my Boy loves me and i
love him. everything is gud. now
eye and Snow Killer and evryone
are all together in the Boy's Room,
living happilee ever after.

And so, by the Grace of the Velveteen, our story is over.

*But the next one begins tomorrow night, as the eternal
fight against the Darkness continues....*

Epilogue: Pro Skills!
By Clark (and Anna and
Grandma Machen)

I've learned a lot from my friends, but Grandma is the master. (Obviously! She made Foon.) Okay, and Anna did a lot of research to make her little pin guy and also a frowny storm cloud Stuffy for her best friend. Anyway, here are some ideas from all three of us (but mostly me and Grandma) to help you boss your sewing. Ready to level up?

The Backstitch

While the running stitch is easy, it's not particularly strong. To make a Stuffy that lasts (and can take some Monster damage without falling apart) you need to use the **backstitch** when sewing by hand.

1. Thread a needle and knot it. Push it up through the layers of fabric from beneath, pulling gently until the knot settles against the cloth.

2. Stick the needle back down through the cloth *in the opposite direction from where you want your seam to go.* That is, if you're following a line to the left, go a half centimeter to the right, and vice versa. That's why it's the *back*stitch, get it? It's kind of *back*ward!

---

3. Push the needle back up through the cloth a half centimeter away from your *first* needle hole, in the direction you *want* to be sewing in.

4. Now put it back down through the cloth next to your first stitch (but not in the same hole as your first stitch), filling in the gap.

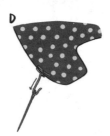

5. Repeat steps 3 and 4 until you are done.

Essentially you are drawing a connected series of loops through the cloth with the thread.

When you're finished, give the seam a test tug. See how much stronger it is? Bonus: There's no gap between stitches you made accidentally too big, where Stuffing could come through.

Fake Fur

The downsides? Expensive and hard to work with. The upside? It's furry!!!

- Always look in the scraps bin at craft and fabric stores for fur remnants—you may luck out on a bargain. Also consider secondhand or thrift stores in the winter coat section. One leopard-print duster could provide enough material to make a whole army of angry, fanged kittens. . . .
- When cutting fake fur, make sure the fur lies in the direction you want it to on the final Stuffy. In other words, don't accidentally cut out a front body piece only to realize that the fur "lies" up, giving your Stuffy a permanently shocked, finger-in-a-socket look.
- If the fur is especially long, try to brush it away from the line where you are going to cut or sew.
- And speaking of cutting, be aware of just how messy it is. Fake fur bits will get *everywhere*.
- After sewing, go over your seams with a comb or brush and pull free any fake fur caught in the stitches. This will give your Stuffy a clean finish.

Safety Eyes

Assuming a Lomer doesn't get them, safety eyes make an extremely professional-looking Stuffy. They come in all sizes, although you might need to order them online to get the specific size you want. Each eye comes with two parts: the rounded eye at the end of what looks a bit like a screw (or an eyestalk), and a doughnut-shaped washer.

- Make a tiny (TINY!) hole in the fabric where you want the eye to be.
- Push the screwy bit in all the way to the wrong side of the fabric so the eye sits on top of the right side of the fabric.
- Put the washer with the sharp points facing down, toward the fabric, and push it as far as you can until it basically locks with the eye. Done!

Kawaii Style

It's not really my thing, but my sister really loves cute (mostly evil) Stuffies. To get that distinctive look it helps to sketch your Stuffy's face out first.

- Remember to space the two eyes pretty far apart. Safety eyes are great for this.
- You can add sewn-on eyelashes at the corners if you want.
- Draw a tiny smiley mouth on the same horizontal level as the eyes so the bottom of the smile just barely dips below the bottom-most points of the eyes.
- Pink cheek circles can be added beneath and a little to the outside of the eyes.
- To get a really soft effect use a light markor or even a little blt of real makeup for them.

Also keep in mind that the Stuffy's head should be reeeallllly large, as large as the body sometimes.

Appendages Stuffed Separately

Are you a little tired of your Stuffies looking flat, but aren't quite ready to launch into making a more complicated 3-D guy? Cutting, sewing, and stuffing the tail, ears, legs, and arms separately and *then* sewing them into the body gives a really nice leveled-up look. **THE TRICK**: When you are ready to sew the body, align the ends of where the (already sewed and stuffed)

appendages will be sewn to the body on the right side of the front body fabric (the side with the Stuffy's face), but *point the appendages to the middle of the body*. Like, if you're adding triangle kitty ears, point them so the tips of the triangles are in the middle of the kitty's face, and the bases are aligned with where your outside seam will be (a little bit of masking tape may help here, to keep everything in place). This allows you to sew around the body neatly. Place the other piece of body fabric on top of this (right side of cloth down) like a sandwich with the appendages as the filling, and sew around the outside, leaving a gap for turning and stuffing. Then when you turn it right side out for stuffing, the ears, arms, etc., should pop up properly in the right positions.

Happy Stuffing!

Acknowledgments

This is a book that has been gestating inside the deep recesses of my head for twenty years. It is now seeing the light of day thanks to my wonderful agent, Ginger Clark, who *got* it immediately. She also gets me, and gets lots of my e-mails, I mean *lots* of them, with the patience of a truly noble Stuffy—with a very high MPF.

Turn the page for a sneak peek
at the sequel to *Stuffed!*

INTO DARKNESS

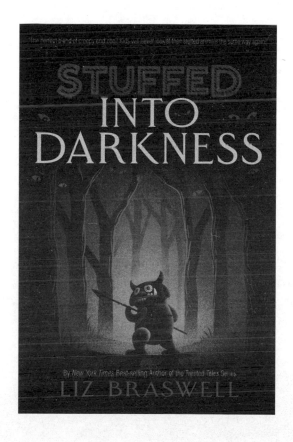

ONE

Here

"I don't think this is a good idea," Clark whispered.

"You *always* don't think *anything* is a good idea," D. A. said. But his voice may have cracked a little. "It's just dark. That doesn't *mean* there's anything down there to get us. Besides, we've got our weapons."

"D. A.'s right," Catherine-Lucille said grimly. "And anyway there's no other choice. Let's just go down the stairs and face whatever's there. Together."

"If we have to," Clark said with a sigh of resignation.

"The stairs are moist with the slimy blood and entrails of whatever came before," Anna told them. The candle flickered, casting ugly shadows around her face. "A cold breeze brings mist and the stench of something long dead—no, worse than that; something still half-alive.

"Or . . . *undead!*"

"ANNA!"

The bright overhead light snapped on, its chilly modern bulb illuminating every corner of the bedroom perfectly. The three kids—and one kid on a video screen—looked up guiltily as Mrs. Smith stood in the doorway, glowering at them.

"How many times have I told you? *No real candles in your room!*"

"We need it for the mood," Anna argued.

"Aw, Mom, we were just about to kick some zombie butt!" Clark grumbled, throwing down his pencil.

"Oh yeah, you sounded *so* thrilled about it." On the video call, Catherine-Lucille rolled her eyes.

"I'm a halfling thief," he pointed out. "We're not known for our bravery. I was playing true to character."

"Sorry, Mrs. Smith," D. A. said, pulling his cap down over his eyebrows. While the gesture was supposed to show that he really *was* sorry, Clark was pretty sure his friend knew its effect on adults, especially moms. They found it adorable and forgave him immediately. Clark wished he had a superpower like that.

"Guess we'll save the zombies for another time," Anna said— with a side-wink at Clark. This meant: *When Mom and Dad are out.*

"We have perfectly realistic battery-operated tea lights you can use," Mrs. Smith said, not quite catching the byplay, but obviously aware via that some kind of silent communication was going on. She narrowed her eyes and blew a puff of hair out of her face. It was a new style, longer and more tendril-y than the bangs-and-tight-ponytail she used to sport. Her job was changing in some way Clark didn't fully understand and now required face-to-face meetings, not just phone calls (she wanted to look *hip* but *trustworthy*, she said).

"I should probably go, anyway," D. A. said with a yawn. "B-ball practice tomorrow morning."

Clark wilted, disappointed that the game was ending so early. Even after they figured out how to bring Catherine-Lucille in, it had been hard to schedule everyone—and then to wheedle Anna into DMing. He picked up the green and gold dice that were D. A.'s birthday present to him and shoved them into their green velvet bag a little harder than necessary.

"Aw, buck up, Private," Catherine-Lucille's pixelated face said. "We'll see each other for real in a few days!"

"That's true," Clark said, brightening. It was more like ten days, but then the three of them would be heading to Camp I Can together for *two whole weeks.* Which meant they would be there for the special intersession camping trip! On the weekend between the two one-week sessions a small number of campers got to hike Mount Wantastiquet and spend the night at the peak, in tents.

(Clark kept the now-worn brochure in his pocket at all times.)

He was not unaware of the complete one-eighty of his feelings on the matter. Last summer he had fought tooth and nail against being forced to go to the camp known for *developing self-esteem* and *fostering independence.* It was the second-worst clash between him and his mom ever.

The reasons he didn't want to go were many and complicated.

It wasn't just because he had never spent a night away from home before. It wasn't even because Stuffies weren't allowed at camp and he had to sneak in the one his grandma had made (Foon, of course). Or the fact that Probably the Best Grandma in the Universe had started chemo for her cancer that same week.

Mostly it was because his dad was slowly being drained by the King Derker who had haunted their house. Clark hadn't wanted to leave his dad alone without constant Stuffy protection.

(But also his mom had used Clark's absence as a chance to try and get rid of his Stuffies.)

(That was the cause of their *first*-worst clash of all time.)

Eventually everything turned out all right, of course. Clark's new friend Catherine-Lucille helped him find an illegal phone the counselors kept hidden in the woods. He used it to call Anna and make sure she was maintaining a Stuffy army around the house every night (she wasn't—but only because his Stuffies had been bagged up and put in the basement). When he finally got home, Foon made short work of the Monster.

(At least it seemed that way: Clark found Foon the next morning all torn up from what looked like a pretty fierce battle. And his dad suddenly began acting normal again. Coincidence? Unlikely. Plus, there were all those weird Stuffy eyes scattered across the basement floor. . . .)

Grandma Machen had taught Clark how to fix Foon, stitch by stitch, while he kept her company at the hospital during her chemo. Both patients recovered completely and were soon back in action. Clark's dad, free from the terrible King Derker, also regained his health, and even took the family to a monster-truck rally—without, ironically, understanding that it was a Monster that had been making him sick.

Anyway, this summer was different. Clark was no longer terrified of being alone, far from home. His parents were now completely safe. He and D. A. might be in the same cabin, Catherine-Lucille would be a short walk away. It would be like one never-ending playdate!

During the school year the three friends had texted, called, video-chatted, Discorded, *every*thinged, but it wasn't the same. Even when they managed to meet up a couple times in real life it was always awkward, at least at the beginning. Besides the usual not-seeing-a-friend-for-a-while uncomfortableness there was also the added bonus of parents being there. They made everything weirder.

Now the three friends would have two whole weeks together! Without parents. *And* a camping trip!

Clark had always been intrigued by the Boy Scouts—from a distance. He loved the idea of earning badges (real ones that you sewed on, not in-game ones), and bonfires and marshmallows and stargazing. It was the "lots of other boys he didn't know or who might not like him" part that wasn't thrilling. Here he would get a bonfire, a tent, and stars—but with his best friends.

No badge, though.

That was kind of a shame.

Clark helped Anna and D. A. pick up all the bits and pieces of a really good D&D campaign: dice, pencils, character sheets, candy wrappers, popcorn and chip bags, miniature pewter figurines, empty Japanese soda bottles.

"Hey, you guys see that video that's been going around?" Catherine-Lucille asked from her screen the moment Anna left the room. "The one of the kid taken over by the Shawgrath?"

"No! Put it on!" D. A. said eagerly.

Clark was…less eager. He knew it was important to stay up-to-date on the world of Monsters and keep himself educated about them. But it was still scary. His dad had almost been devoured by a Monster. Sometimes he wished he could go back to wondering if they were real—wondering, instead of *knowing*.

"Here." Catherine-Lucille's fingers moved below the screen and a link popped up beside her face. D. A. clicked it and turned up the volume.

At first it was hard to see anything, like all of the videos of this type. A dark room with strange things gleaming or glowing in the infrared of the night camera. Squinting, Clark could just make out the outlines of a bed and someone sleeping in it.

Suddenly the kid sat up.

Her eyes shone white in the black-and-white world—and she didn't blink.

She just sat up and stared, like a confused zombie.

"Aw, that's nothing," D. A. said disappointedly. "Just some little kid who had a nightmare or has to pee or something."

"Shh. Watch!" Catherine-Lucille ordered.

After a few moments of stillness the girl in the video got

out of bed—jerkily, like a puppet. She stood in the middle of the room and again stayed frozen, doing nothing. Then she whirled suddenly, lurched over to the corner of her room, looked up—and *began talking*.

There was no sound, of course. Her lips moved and her eyes shone like she was having a serious conversation with the cobwebs—or Cowbers—on the ceiling.

Then, as she spoke, something—her breath, a shadow, a thin stream of vapor—began to seep out of her mouth.

"Pause it," Clark ordered. D. A. did so without hesitation. "Go back, like, a half second and enlarge the screen."

There was no doubt about it.

The stuff coming out of her mouth wasn't like the fog on a cold day. It was stringy and sticky-looking, long threads like a parachute spider might spin before floating away on a morning breeze. If that web was a foot long and inside a girl's head.

"Oh man," D. A. said in wonder. "That's so weird! And . . . disgusting."

"*Definitely* a Shawgrath. Or maybe an Ergootz," Catherine-Lucille said thoughtfully. "Like, a tiny one."

"Why weren't there videos like this before?" Clark demanded. "I mean, you're finding them all the time now, and before I met you I'd never seen a single one."

"That's because you didn't even know to look for them. Or what to look for," D. A. said with a laugh. "Plus, this is C. L. here. She's the Monster Expert."

"No, that's actually a good point," the *Expert* said unexpectedly. "There *do* seem to be more and more sightings and posts."

"Yeah, by accounts like . . ." D. A. leaned in to read the name of the video's creator. "'Akidsbedtimestory.' It could totally be a fake."

"Who would make a little kid act out something so scary?" Clark wondered. Not a good parent. Not even a halfway decent big sister. Anna had done a lot of questionable things, but nothing that put Clark into a potentially nightmare-inducing situation.

"A jerk who wants to make a lot of money off the internet," D. A. suggested. "Okay, guys. I gotta jet. We can totally discuss all this at camp, though."

"Gonna be hard," Catherine-Lucille said, tapping her tooth in thought. "Since we can't show videos. We can only trade notes. The club should come up with a system for ranking videos by how believable they are, and how trustworthy the sources."

"Hey, uh . . ." Clark cleared his throat. He didn't want to sound like a baby, or a beggar, or desperate. "So . . . uh . . . about the club . . ."

"Oh, Clark, relax," Catherine-Lucille said with one of her rare smiles. "You're in. We'll properly induct you the first night we formally meet. Okay? Stop worrying so much. You're with me. You're in. *HEY*, idiot, that's *my* cupcake!"

It took both boys a moment to realize she wasn't yelling at them, but at someone at her house, off-screen.

Anna popped her head back into the room. "Clark? Mom says you gotta wipe the table and sweep and then go take a shower."

"Sigh. Okay. See you later, C. L."

Clark closed the "Catherine-Lucille" computer; she was already gone and yelling at one of her cousins.

D. A. grabbed his bike helmet. "I'll see you online when I get home."

"Yeah, at least until nine," Clark said, walking him downstairs. They bumped knuckles at the front door, drawing their hands out afterward and wiggling their fingers like tentacles.

The sun was just setting. An orange spill of syrupy light spread out behind the houses across the street. Bright pink clouds stood out against the trees, their topmost branches as dark as the darkest, most starless night.

Clark felt a strange mixture of things. Wonder at the beauty of the sunset. Relief he no longer feared the night quite as much as he had.

(Why would he, now that he knew for certain that his Stuffies protected him?)

He watched D. A. pedal down the dim street, the only noise the *swischt* of his rubber tires against the sidewalk. His headlight bobbed up and down like a will-o' the-wisp going out, getting smaller and smaller until it disappeared.

Clark was torn between envy that the other boy was allowed the privilege of biking at night and a strange wistfulness he couldn't name. Something about lights dimming into the distance. Something about summer ending, even though it was only the beginning of August.

He turned and went back in, deciding to get ready for bed early.

TWO

Here, Night

If an adult staying up for the late-late show had not been lulled to sleep by the magic of the Moon—and had looked out the window—she would have seen a strange sight.

Two groups of small, lumpy objects outside, under the streetlights, moved a little when they probably shouldn't have.

They seemed to be interacting.

It would be hard to tell at that distance what the things were made of: there were no sharp angles, no smooth sides, no shiny facets of plastic or metal or rock.

Foon, Hero of the Basement, Emissary of the Light, Ground Commander of House Clark, was shaking the hand—wing— of Dredful Duck of House Maya. Over the property line that divided their two realms, as was customary. Accompanying the duck was her cohort: Macow, Aramdillo, Dog, and Frank. With

Foon were Winkum, Draco, Fang, Bo Bear, Dark Horse, and Kevin.

"We thank you for all your help," Dredful said, bowing deeply. Her bill almost touched the grass. It was worn through right to the Stuffing. She was loved, very much indeed, and therefore worthy of the greatest respect. She easily had an MPF of ten—which was pretty amazing for a duck. "It was a terrible infestation; I don't know how long it would have taken us to clear out that nest of Sorvors."

"I'm sure you could have accomplished the task yourself in time," Foon said generously. "But we were honored to be asked to help."

He too bowed, saluting her with the tip of his trident Focus as his soft sock-body bent in half. It was a graceful, elegant gesture and all of House Maya were suitably impressed by it and his words.

"I am concerned, however..." the duck added thoughtfully. "We do a routine House check and perimeter search every night—I don't know how that nest even got built there without our noticing. And it was a corner of the attic closest to *your* house. The vent practically overlooks your second floor."

"Is it not usual for Sorvors to nest in dark and lonely attics?" Foon asked.

"Yes, but... news of your renown has spread far and wide, friend," the duck said with a twinkle in her eye. "If I were a

Sorvor, I would want to nest as far away from *your* House as possible. You are death to Monsters. Unless there was some other reason for it."

Foon bowed his head humbly. "You do me great honor, Dredful Duck. But Monsters have no thought or plan or reason. I am just glad I was able to rid you of their foul presence."

"Oh, absolutely, Foon. That is what's truly important here. Henceforth let there be an alliance between our Houses. For where there is Light..."

"There is always Dark," Foon finished.

They gravely saluted and parted, each group of Stuffies returning to their own Houses.

Those of House Clark hopped one on top of another and made a tall, swaying tower that reached the doorknob of the Front Door. After a little wrangling they finally managed to open it, tumbling inside in a happy pile of softness. Not Foon: He did a flip on the way down and landed on his paws, ready to spring back into action if anything threatened.

Nothing did, of course. His House was a sanctuary, a beacon of the Light.

His friends were in high spirits.

"Let us cut through the kitchen and say hello to the Ap-Lionses!" Kevin cried. The small beanbag polar bear was always a little more outgoing than the rest, perhaps because Clark carried him around the Outside so much.

The Stuffies marched in line, chanting:

Yarn and thread and fur and string
We will fight most anything
Moon and stars and needle and pin
We will fight and we will win!

"What ho, little Stuffies!" the Espresso Maker called genially from above. "Victory, was it?"

"An entire clutch of Sorvors!" Bo Bear called back in his surprisingly deep voice. He was small and very light green.

"We freed House Maya of their Monsters; it is now a complete sanctuary of the Light," Foon explained.

"Well done, all, well done!" the Blender cried, whirring his blades.

All the Ap-Lionses made noises of congratulations: clicking, clinking, beeping, and grinding. The Stuffies waved and laughed and marched through while blue and white and green lights flashed on and off like a fireworks display.

Foon smiled, watching his friends enjoy their moment of triumph. But his smile faded when they passed the basement door. He shivered, remembering the Lomer, and the eyes, and the well-spoken but evil King Derker who almost killed him.

Even after they won, it was months before Foon could speak or think properly again. His injuries were extreme.

The Stuffies marched quickly on through the living room and turned to go upstairs. A few Dust Pugs, delighted by the show, joined in the parade, bouncing and rolling along behind. They all marched down the hall and into the Boy's Room.

Snowy had been left in charge; the owl clapped her giant wings twice in greeting.

"Well met, Foon! I assume from all the noise you have had a great success!"

"Well met, Snow Killer! We have indeed! With any luck, we shall soon have this entire neighborhood free of the Dark, a safe haven for all who stay in the Light!"

"That would be a mighty thing indeed," Winkum, the oldest, most loved horse said with a kind smile. "But let us celebrate our current victories now, and think of the future later."

"Of course," Foon said quickly, ashamed of his boastful words. Of course they should honor the bravery and accomplishments of his comrades tonight, and not belittle them by focusing on the greater war and the future instead.

Winkum was so very, very wise. Foon wondered if there would ever come a day when *he* would have as much wisdom to bestow on younger Stuffies. It didn't seem possible.